SYLVIA

SYLVIA

Maithreyi Karnoor

Neem Tree
PRESS

Published by Neem Tree Press Limited 2023

Copyright © Maithreyi Karnoor, 2023

Neem Tree Press Limited
95A Ridgmount Gardens, London, WC1E 7AZ
info@neemtreepress.com
www.neemtreepress.com

A catalogue record for this book is available from the British Library
ISBN 978-1-915584-03-8 Paperback
ISBN 978-1-915584-04-5 Ebook

Printed and bound in Great Britain

For Rhys Hughes

CONTENTS

Part I

BHAUBAAB

"As *dodda hunasemara*, the large tamarind tree of Savanur
Brought as seed across the seas to a new peninsula
And welded to this earth through centuries and centuries
As one being, the baobab, scoffing at the tall tale of life,
Looks heavenwards and thirst, thirst, thirstily
Claws at the dry blue sky, mining moisture of memory
Of home; its trunk swollen with the waters of longing
For belonging since an age when time was measured in kings
And the land marked by the lack of cartography.

"When things lack names in a new language, they are lent the names of others that are the closest fit. Like borrowed pyjamas when one stays overnight with a friend one is visiting for dinner. It means the drink and the conversation lasts longer than expected. The ill-fitting clothes are markers of a happy time. When the baobabs arrived from faraway Africa to the arid plains of the Deccan 1,800 years ago, took root in the saline soil of Savanur and grew up as trees that lacked a name in Kannada, they were simply called Large Tamarind Trees. These living beings have stood transfixed by changing times, living past capacities of human memory until no one remembered who brought them there. Until they were worshipped – and hence accepted and protected."

Sylvia read aloud to herself the words she had written on her laptop. She had quit her job to travel and write about places and people. She felt confident that she could pitch this story, about the mysterious baobab trees in a village in central Karnataka, to an international travel magazine with a literary bent. It was a good story.

*

Bhaubaab was not his real name. As Cajetan Pereira, he would have fitted in without a batted eyelid in the little south-Goan village, when he arrived there, a while ago. Even though his name, skin colour, religion, and even his expat status were markers of a deep Goanness, there was something about him that didn't quite conform to this unique, seemingly monolithic, but highly layered identity.

It was not the fact that he spoke no Konkani, as many expats didn't. But, while the returning expat always came back seeking their ancestral village, Cajetan did not actually trace his roots to this one – or even to this area. It was, in fact, from Bardez, in the north, that Mateus Pereira, his grandfather, had left Goa for Africa. He had no old, high-ceilinged home with mother-of-pearl windows that was lying locked and overgrown, that he creaked open and laid claim to in this south-Goan village. His wish to buy a house and settle there, with no ostensible purpose, made the villagers wary and kept them from welcoming him with arms as wide open as they normally would. Also, he spoke little, and his shyness was mistaken for aloofness. To the gregarious Goan villager, that is something to be suspicious about. Still, he was a Goan, after all, so he was a brother, a *bhau*, and a respectable elder, a *baab*. And Bhaubaab is what he became.

The real-estate agent he had hired to find him a house when he first arrived had thought of comfort and practicality when he showed him the few newer buildings with modern fittings that the village had. They were all close to the village centre, with its 400-year-old church, a post office of much lesser antiquity, several grocery and liquor shops, a Marwari sweet shop, a convention hall that had regular *tiatr* shows, and a concrete-roofed marketplace that sold fish, vegetables, beef and Goan sausages. But Bhaubaab had rejected them all without a second thought. He had gone around asking for a large tree. Not many knew what he was talking about, but when he showed them a picture of a baobab, with its swollen trunk and furry oval fruit that looked like a miniature jackfruit with fuzzy skin, someone recognised it and walked him through boggy paddy fields to a slightly high-lying, rocky place where the said tree stood. It had been marked off by a protective fence. He stood there looking at it in silence. Although his face betrayed no emotion, the length of his gaze seemed to suggest he had arrived home. "Are there any houses to be had nearby?" Bhaubaab had enquired. There was a house, he was told, just below the rising on the other side, which had not been lived in for decades and needed extensive repair before anyone could move in. The agent couldn't see why he would want it, but Bhaubaab had stood on its veranda to assure himself of the baobab's visibility from there, and had insisted on having it.

The legal owner of the house took some tracing, as the man who had built it had died childless long ago. His brother's only surviving grandson had lived in Navelim most of his life and had lost his bakery to drink and finally moved to the sea, where he had a shack on an unpopular part of the beach in Varca. When the real-estate agent came looking for him, he was staring glassily at the waves over his *feni* and Limca and thinking about the time when he could have sailed off as a cook on these very waters, as most of his friends had; but he loved his football too much to give up land for water and prosperity. And prosperity had eluded him ever since. He gave up on his dreams of becoming a professional footballer when his father suddenly died and he had to work as a *poder* to support his mother and four sisters. The bakery he eventually saved up to buy did not last in his ownership for too long, as he quickly lost the heart to run it and began drowning his sorrows in *feni*. He was taken by surprise when he was told he owned a house in his ancestral village. But he recovered sufficiently, and fast enough, to quote a ridiculously high price and chase the agent away.

When his wife in Pune found out what was going on, she took two nights off from work, bought the last ticket on an overnight Kadamba Volvo and came to look at the house that her husband suddenly owned. She talked him into accepting half of what he had asked for. "Even that is a generous price for it. It is money we didn't know we had, remember?" She could finally give up her call-centre job and return home to be with her children. "The night shifts are wreaking havoc on my periods and God knows I will be drained dry soon if I keep this up, man." With that money, they could perhaps fix their house and take in foreign boarders during the season. He could even buy a car and run a taxi for tourists. After finalising the deal, she got on the next Kadamba back to serve a month's notice before she could quit. She would have to pay the multinational company she worked for a month's salary to get her papers of release if she quit right away.

Bhaubaab bought the house and began fixing it. This was not one of those large bungalows that belong to prominent families and get featured in nostalgia pieces in magazines or architectural journals, or even tourism catalogues catering to the elite traveller; one whose upkeep is a financial nightmare. It had belonged to a *sudir* man of modest means who had endeavoured to put a roof above his head in the only fashion it was done in his time – the generic Goan home. Real estate didn't mean a whole lot back then and space had not been a constraint. In fact, most houses belonging to even the poorest families of the earlier generations in Goa felt lavishly roomy to city folks who were used to claustrophobic living.

The original construction of Bhaubaab's new house had only two very large, high-ceilinged rooms, with a long veranda in the front covered by the overhang of the sloping roof. There had been two mutually facing mortar *sopos* on each side of the veranda and about two or three steps that ran down from it to the ground below. The kitchen had obviously been a separate enclosure at the back, and the bathing and toilet areas must have been different, detached structures. At some later point, the old owner had probably renovated the building according to more modern tastes by pulling down the kitchen and toilet and adding two more rooms, box-like, right behind the existing ones, along with a narrow kitchen and a modern bathroom behind them, joined together like railway coaches. The original roof had been a rectangular pyramid over the first two rooms, and the newer additions had been given a roof that sloped on two sides, extended to touch the first roof to ensure no open spaces. This new construction was also old by current standards, and Bhaubaab had to pay a plumber to have a toilet bowl, a wash basin and a shower fixed in the enclosure that had been the bathroom. He even had another small bathroom, with the necessary fixtures, built in one of the older rooms and made it his master bedroom. The kitchen needed covered storage spaces to keep the supplies from becoming rat-fodder. The long table in one of the newer rooms, which was obviously a dining space, needed polishing, and one of the legs needed a few nails to keep it upright. But, most importantly, a majority of the ceiling tiles needed to be replaced. The ones that hadn't cracked were overgrown with weeds and crammed with leaf litter and moss, which, instead of letting the rainwater run down over them, allowed it to seep through. Thankfully, the monsoons were months away and Bhaubaab did not have to suffer water damage to his belongings.

A truckload of Mangalore tiles was ordered, and soon the roof went from the dark grey and black of dry mould to an even rust-red, making the house look like a wrinkly old man wearing a colourful new hat. The outer walls, a dirty off-white, had apparently been yellow at one time. Bhaubaab decided to retain the shade and had them painted bright yellow with white borders around the large windows and on the pillars. The inner walls were whitewashed with a lime-based paint. The house suddenly lit up like a jolly okra flower resplendent as it would be in the rare beam of sun through the clouds in full monsoon. There was a decrepit, triangular altar in a corner of the living room, which held a crucifix, an idol of Mother Mary with one hand raised in blessing, and a couple of saints he couldn't identify. He had stopped praying long before the phrase "spiritual but not religious" was popular, but he had the broken glass cabinet of the altar replaced for aesthetic reasons.

The well in the backyard had plenty of water, but he had been advised against drinking it. While well water was the only water in the whole village and had, long ago, been clean and safe, it had started to acquire a strange smell in recent years. Though the smell was only slight, people had associated it with the ever-growing landfill a short distance from the village. The infamous hill of stench had alarmed the villagers, and they were worried the garbage was seeping into the ground and mixing with their groundwater. So, they had stopped drinking the water from their wells, even as all their plastic ended up on the same hill. They considered the well water to be fine for baths and the garden. But, for drinking, they relied on the municipal water supply. Bhaubaab's house had not had a water connection for years, as it had ceased to be inhabited back when well water was still deemed fit for drinking. He made a formal request at the *panchayat*, but was told it would take a while for the pipes to be laid. The tall weeds growing in the well – some of which were almost small trees – were cleared and he fitted an electric pump in it to draw water for domestic use.

While Bhaubaab's house was getting a facelift, many curious villagers dropped by to look at it – and to meet the house's mysterious new owner. One of them was Lakshmi – short for Lakshminarayan Shetty – a shy young man in his early twenties, with film-star good looks. He was Bhaubaab's closest neighbour. The backyard of his house was visible from Bhaubaab's compound through half an acre of thick undergrowth. The space was most certainly overrun with snakes and he had to circumnavigate the area and take a longer path to reach Bhaubaab's house. Lakshmi had been taking small bottles of drinking water from his house for Bhaubaab while the renovation was underway. He offered to bring him larger quantities – twenty-litre bottles – on his scooter until the municipal connection materialised.

The villagers, having decided that Bhaubaab's Western upbringing was to blame for his introversion, had tried to facilitate a proper return home for him with cleansing banter. Though never impolite, he found their endeavours tiring and, therefore, found himself warming to Lakshmi, who was almost as reticent as himself.

Lakshmi was homebound since his return from Bangalore after failing to get into Kannada films. There were whispers about a tragic dam incident which had left him traumatised and hastened his return to the little Goan village that reciprocated the rest of the world's ignorance of it with equal nonchalance. Lakshmi was the fourth son of his parents, and after his birth they had given up seeking the coveted daughter to fulfil the propensities of their matrilineal community. He had, nonetheless, tried to placate them with his delicate features and smooth skin, which stood in sharp contrast with his brothers' sturdy dark builds of solid *Bunt* stock. He had been the target of gentle ribbing as his mother dressed him in frilly frocks and tied ribbons in his long soft hair as a young child.

Although he gave up dresses and ribbons and cropped his hair close like the rest of his brothers when he started school, he wasn't spared the ridicule of his classmates for being too pretty for a boy. It didn't help that his name was shortened to Lakshmi, which only referred to the consort of the god he was named after – a god who was happy being identified as the husband of the goddess of wealth. He fought with his classmates to get them to call him Narayan instead, but they wouldn't give him that pleasure.

While his brothers scraped through exams and played football and swam in the comunidade ponds, Lakshmi scored above-average marks in school and sulked around at home playing board games with his mother – when she had any free time from running a home of nearly half a dozen men. He had shown a fair amount of academic inclination, but no one knew what to do with it.

His father had migrated to Goa from their native village near Kundapura, in coastal Karnataka, as a young boy apprenticed to an uncle in the restaurant business in Colva. He had stayed on in Goa, started his own restaurant and married a distant cousin before settling down in the village they now lived in. The family spoke Tulu at home and Konkani outside, and although in the early days they had spoken with some vigour about "going back home" after saving up, the utterance of that plan had turned more religious in the sense of being reduced to a noncommittal ritual over the years, as they had son after son in the village, built a house and formed abiding friendships there.

Lakshmi's brothers dropped out of school at the age of fourteen, helped their father in the business, learned the trade and branched out on their own before their respective twenty-first birthdays. One of them moved to Savordem, where his bar, catering to the mining truck drivers, was doing good business. Another moved to north Goa and became a manager in a floating casino, and would soon begin eyeing it more ambitiously. The third brother remained in the village to help his father and to ensure that the business remained steady.

Lakshmi, meanwhile, had gone on to complete his twelfth standard with good grades, which was more to do with the fact that nobody had paid him any notice when he didn't drop out, rather than any great familial back-patting on his achievement. Since their finances were running as smoothly as desired, Lakshmi's lack of contribution to the household wasn't of any concern to his parents. But, beyond that, no one knew what he must do with himself. By the time he left school, he had grown up to be a very good-looking young man. He was tall and light-skinned. He let his straight hair grow out a few inches and, when it fell on his eyes, he flicked it back with a jerk of his head in a way that charmed to the viscera everyone around. His face was oval and his dimples deep. The transparent quality of his honey-coloured eyes under long lashes seemed to be hiding mischievous thoughts behind that mock pellucidity, and the girls in his class felt a strange warmth around their ears whenever his gaze brushed past them. When it fell on his mother, she sighed aloud, wondering why he couldn't have been a girl, a true "Lakshmi of our home".

Thus, made aware of his good looks by all the women he knew, Lakshmi yearned for more attention – larger, more worthwhile attention. When he found out that a distant cousin in Bangalore was acting in Kannada films, Lakshmi wanted to join him and try his luck. His parents thought it a good idea too. With three sons following in the family trade, why not spare a fourth to walk a path that was not yet beaten in their family? It would be nice to have a film-star son.

When Lakshmi arrived in Bangalore on the Velankanni Express, he was greeted by his cousin and his room-mate, a fellow denizen of the Kannada film industry popularly known as "Sandalwood". They were men who took their gym seriously. They were also pleasant and warm and welcomed Lakshmi with "yo-bro" affable punches and hugs. Lakshmi followed them to their tiny home, where they cooked and ate in the first room and unrolled their mattresses and slept in the other one. When he had set his bags down and looked around the place, which was sandwiched between a slum and a vegetarian middle-class neighbourhood, it had dawned on Lakshmi that his cousin and his friend were strugglers in the industry. They worked as stuntmen, in fact. Their routine consisted of working out in the gym several hours a day, cooking and eating chicken, and heading off to jump from tall buildings, run through fire or ride motorcycles off ramps.

Since Lakshmi had the looks, they were hopeful of him getting cushier roles that involved more heart and cash than muscle and small change. They advised him not to go overboard with upper-body workouts: heroes must have just enough muscle to convince the audience that they could beat the hell out of beefy villains, but not so much that they would scare off the delicate heroines. "You have the face for it. Don't lose it with brawn. Do more cardio and easy toning exercises to stay in shape." He was also advised to join a theatre group. "Do a workshop, go on stage, do a few plays, meet people and press your case. Theatre and film circles are closely connected. If you land roles – big or small – in TV serials, take them. It is a slow process, but perseverance is important. You are cute. You have a chance." What about them, then? "We are too burly, and our faces are too rugged for us to ever land lead roles. But we are optimistic about making it big in negative roles. In fact, we are in talks with some very important people and, if everything works out right, we might land roles in this big movie that will make our careers. It involves some pretty scary stunts, but, with it, we will arrive on the dark side of Kannada Tinseltown."

Lakshmi set about working on the plan marked out by his two room-mates, who were now his *annas*, older brothers. He joined a theatre group whose director had close connections with cinema personalities. He joined a gym, but was careful to keep his physique boyish and easily loveable. But the biggest challenge for him was language. Although his family came from Karnataka, Kannada was not their language and, unlike his cousin who had lived all his life in Mangalore and Bangalore, he'd had no reason to learn the official state language. Rather than join a class, Lakshmi began learning Kannada by watching films.

Four months into this routine, he was making slow but steady headway. His Kannada was getting better by the day, his theatre director's niece – whose uncle on the other side of the family was the highest-paid character actor in Kannada cinema – had a crush on him, and his first play, a Kannada adaptation of *Hamlet* in which he played the eponymous role of Hemalathan, was being staged next week. The entire cast consisted of novices just like him, hence they were opening in a small-time auditorium near Lalbagh. If they did well, they would do a rerun in Ranga Shankara, the centre of Kannada theatre in Bangalore, and, a week after that, at the Shakespeare festival, which was scheduled to be graced by a famous film director who was known to be on the lookout for a fresh face for his upcoming detective-thriller-love-triangle.

Lakshmi was excited. His mother was travelling to Bangalore to watch him on stage for the first time. It seemed to be a lucky time, for his beloved annas had finally landed their pivotal roles too. They were to do their stunts on a helicopter. They were shivering with excitement about being in a chopper for the first time. The mood was celebratory in anticipation of success all round.

The Lalbagh show went well. Lakshmi shone as Hemalathan. "*Iruvudo, illadiruvudo embudey ee prashne, ghatakaadrushtagala kavane baanagala-nnu sahisuvudu...*" As he delivered the translation of the iconic soliloquy in complicated, Sanskritised Kannada with practised ease and natural aplomb, no one could tell he had only learned the language in the last few months. He knew he was good too. And he was elated. He knew in his heart that the Ranga Shankara show was going to be decisive – that it would change his life. And it did.

On the day of his show, his annas were taken to a large reservoir outside the city and told by the director that the scene involved a daring mid-air fight with the hero and that they would all have to jump from a height of a hundred feet from the helicopter into the water. Neither of them knew how to swim, but it didn't matter. They were assured that they wouldn't spend more than a minute in the water. Don't worry, they were told. There would be a rescue boat waiting to haul them out the moment they touched the water. It was supposed to be their big break. They prayed to their family goddess Durga Parameshwari for courage and jumped to their deaths.

The rescue boat stationed close by couldn't reach them in time, as the strong currents raised by the helicopter's blades kept pushing it away. The hero managed to swim to safety, and the villains he was supposed to fight drowned fighting the water for a snatch of breath. The chicken-fed, bulging muscles on their chests, the superlatively optimistic dreams in their heads of becoming celebrated bad guys were no match for the water's cold and steady denial of air.

Lakshmi was given this news as he readied himself to enter the hallowed Ranga Shankara proscenium, just before Girish Karnad's recorded voice boomed on the speaker asking everyone to silence their phones – first in Kannada and then in English. As the first scene unfolded between Maresha, Harsha and Barindra on the stage, Lakshmi – dressed and made up as Hemalathan – stood shell-shocked in the wings. He did ghost-walk on to the stage on cue in the second scene. But, instead of acting, he let out a heart-rending scream and collapsed on the floor, sobbing hysterically. They had to carry him off the stage in a fireman's lift. With this ended Lakshmi's dreams of covering himself with stardust. He was hospitalised briefly before being sent back home to the village.

*

It was not that Bhaubaab wanted to withhold his story from his new neighbours. He was just not talkative and didn't feel the need to volunteer information. But when someone did ask, he was quite forthcoming in his answers – albeit to the point.

"So, you are not from Salcete, uh?"

"No."

"Where you are from, then?"

"Tanzania."

"Tanzania? Africa?"

"Yes."

"No, no…in Goa, where you are from?"

"My family comes from Aldona."

"But you are born and brought up in Africa only?"

"I lived in Tanzania as a young boy. But my family moved to the UK when I was fourteen. Since then, we lived there."

"Who all are there in your family?"

"Just me. Parents passed away a few years ago. I have an older brother, but I haven't been in touch with him in years. In fact, I don't know anything about his whereabouts."

"Oh? So sad, man. And wife and children?"

"I'm divorced. No children."

"Very sorry to hear. So, you want to come back home for retired life, uh? *Amchem* Goa is *bayst*, no? Wherever you go in the world, Goa is our homeland. But why you are not going back to Aldona only?"

"There's no one there now. Nothing to go 'back' to."

"You don't worry, *baab*. It is *bayst* here. No one will give you any trouble. Nice, peaceful. Anything you want means ask. You are coming to church, no? You are *bamon*?"

"I think so. I'm not sure. My parents never spoke about it."

"It's okay. I'm sure you are. But Mass is in Konkani, uh."

"I intend to learn."

*

This information, which had circulated quickly in the village, is what Lakshmi had come with, curiously peeping into Bhaubaab's house. Lakshmi's parents were relieved that he was stepping out of the house again. It had been months now and he had done nothing but lock himself up in his room and mope around all day. He came out at mealtimes, picked at his rice and fish curry, and went back to lie on his bed and gaze absently at the ceiling. Even his favourite *gujje gasi* couldn't get him interested in his lunch. He had also started waking up several times every night, gasping for breath. His brother in Panjim had taken him to Dr Chodankar, the most celebrated ENT specialist in the state, who had examined him and declared that there was nothing wrong with him physiologically. It seemed like it was a psychological problem caused by trauma of some kind. He suggested they see his colleague in the psychiatric department, but Lakshmi's brother had firmly refused and brought him back home. He just needed good food and fresh air and a little distraction – and time. Not mental doctors pumping him with pills. "Time is best healer, no?"

His father tried talking him into joining him and his brother at the restaurant, but Lakshmi had refused. So, it was a welcome surprise for his parents when that *Afrikar baab* arrived and began redoing that abandoned house behind theirs, arousing Lakshmi's curiosity. He sat up and looked out of the window, and, later in the evening, changed out of his shorts into a pair of jeans and walked over to see for himself what had caused this ripple in the sleepy neighbourhood.

Lakshmi didn't ask pointed questions like the others. He brought drinking water without being asked and Bhaubaab took it without comment. Bhaubaab noticed his good looks. Lakshmi liked the older man's unimposing build – not lean, not fat, but certainly not showing any extra effort in looking a certain way. Thick crop of hair, greying at the temples, small but bulbous nostrils at the end of a long bridge upon which were placed frameless glasses that he pushed down and peered over when speaking at close proximity. Clever but kind eyes, clean-shaven dark skin on a simple square face. Tall. Taller than Lakshmi, who was above average height himself. They studied each other without hunger or hubris. They talked very little in the beginning. Lakshmi simply came and stood around while workers bustled about fixing the house, and they got used to each other's presence.

When Lakshmi told him that his parents had invited him over for tea, Bhaubaab politely declined, saying he wasn't keen on socialising, but he was happy to have Lakshmi over as often and for as long as he wanted. Lakshmi became an intrinsic part of Bhaubaab's home. He came after lunch every day and stayed until late at night. Sometimes, they played Scrabble, Pictionary or Jenga in the living room that Bhaubaab had furnished with a settee, several beanbags and an ornate coffee table on a brightly coloured carpet. Other times, they sat in silence on the *sopo* on the veranda – Bhaubaab looking at the baobab, and Lakshmi following his gaze to settle on the tree too. Sometimes, they had a beer or two together. An easy honesty seemed to flow between these men separated by a few decades. Neither of them sized each other up in words or looks, neither put up pretences to please or subdue the other – neither displayed greater knowledge or a superior sense of self-worth. There was no melancholy or grimness to their mostly wordless communication. They actually smiled at the same things and shared laughter on many occasions.

"Bhaubaab, baobab, Bhaubaab, baobab," Lakshmi began chanting one evening, and Bhaubaab laughed.

"You came here to be named after a tree?"

"That wasn't the idea. I didn't even know such a name was possible. I just wanted to come home."

Lakshmi tossed back the last gulp of beer and leaned back on the *sopo*. He felt today Bhaubaab would tell him more.

"There was a tree like that just outside Dar es Salaam, where I grew up, and I liked it very much. Later, we moved to the UK and I missed it. But going back to Africa was never an option. My mother had always spoken about 'returning home to Goa'. I had visited Aldona as a child a couple of times and had some good memories of it—"

"Aldona? Seen that legend on the cemetery there?" Lakshmi cut him short.

"*Aiz maka falea tuka*? Yes. My mother translated it for me once. Very reassuring."

"Reassuring? The words 'today me, tomorrow you' on a cemetery gate is reassuring to you? Being reminded of the certainty of death is not depressing?"

"On the contrary, it is very freeing. We tend to take everything – love, loss, success, disappointments – too seriously

19

because we forget that the only certain thing about life is death. If we teach ourselves not to forget it, we will take all of these in our stride. They would hurt less – they will elate us less too, but that is the point."

He turned to look at Lakshmi and saw that his eyes had welled up. He put a hand on his shoulder and Lakshmi began weeping. Bhaubaab hugged him gently as he sobbed into his chest.

Lakshmi pulled away after a couple of minutes, wiping his tears. He looked up and smiled weakly at Bhaubaab.

"I'm sorry, I interrupted you. So, you came to Goa looking for the baobab tree of your childhood?"

"Perceptive lad."

"On the one hand, you don't want to forget death. On the other, you want to be near a permanently living being? Permanent by human standards, in any case. It is just subjective vision, I suppose. Nothing is permanent, no? Not the earth, not even the universe."

"There. You said it yourself. Death and permanent life aren't all that different."

"*Iruvudo illadiruvudo embudey ee prashne,*" Lakshmi muttered.

"What is that?"

" 'To be be or not to be, that is the question.' I acted in a Kannada adaptation of *Hamlet* once."

"Oh? Nice, huh?"

"Yes."

When he went home later, Lakshmi found his mother and *attige*, his sister-in-law, sitting on the floor with a large, unripe jackfruit that had been cracked open in the middle with a heavy knife, and a bowl of coconut oil. His mother rubbed the oil on her fingers and skilfully began pulling out the fleshy pulp from under the spiny skin of the fruit.

"*Gujje gasi* for dinner!" Lakshmi exclaimed. His mother looked up at him in delighted surprise.

Bhaubaab had settled in, and Lakshmi began to spend more time in his house than his own. He stayed overnight with him several times a week. His *attige* had recently had a baby and it was a struggle for her to get it to sleep. She would snatch a few winks of sleep herself when the baby slept. If Lakshmi found that the household was quiet when he arrived after his evenings with Bhaubaab, he'd simply go back to his new friend's house rather than wake the baby with his knocking and thus stir up the whole house. His parents didn't mind, as they were quite grateful to Bhaubaab for bringing the sparkle back to their boy's eyes. They thought that their new neighbour's avuncular presence would have a good influence on their son and get him to do something worthwhile with his life.

Like every house there, Bhaubaab's had its own coconut trees. Since the house had been uninhabited the last many, many years, the neighbours used to harvest the coconuts in the trees themselves. When Bhaubaab moved in, they assumed he'd want the trees and their fruits. When they realised that he didn't know what to do with his coconuts, they taught him their methods. They even helped him hire the right man for the job. Now, the storage shed in Bhaubaab's compound was stacked up with unshelled coconuts waiting to be sent off to the oil mill.

That day, Lakshmi's mother had asked him to get a couple of coconuts for the morning chutney from Bhaubaab – their own crop had been sold off to the tender-coconut merchant. Bhaubaab went into the storage shed to get them for him. He carried an LED flashlight as the shed in the backyard was a dungeon-like enclosure that did not get any natural light during the day; the electric wires were broken and he hadn't bothered replacing them. When he bent down to pick a coconut from the large heap, there was a clearly audible hiss. Lakshmi, who was right behind him, thought it must be a cat slinking around in the dark room in search of mice. But Bhaubaab would not be deceived. Nor would he be scared.

"Hello, my friend," he whispered under his breath.

"What? Cat. No?" Lakshmi asked.

"Not cat. Snake."

Lakshmi ran out of the shed screaming. "Come out! I'll go call some men. They'll kill it."

"No," said Bhaubaab calmly, standing still. "We will not kill it. I'll catch it."

"Wha…whatever for?"

"It doesn't need to die just for being in my way," Bhaubaab said. "Go find me a gunny bag – it must be strong – and a two-inch PVC pipe. And a metal hook, if you can find one."

Lakshmi looked bewildered, but went about looking for the prescribed items.

It's strange how one finds all kinds of things lying around houses that haven't been inhabited in a long time. There are discarded knick-knacks from the last inhabitants, things dumped by the hangers-on that such places inevitably attract, and garbage thrown by people trying to declutter their own homes. Although Bhaubaab's home had undergone much cleaning and renovation, the paraphernalia of abandonment hadn't been completely cleared yet. It had merely been bundled up and dumped in a corner of the large backyard and left there to miraculously shed its problematic character.

Lakshmi managed to find a hook, a pipe and a sack, all fitting the description of Bhaubaab's demands, among a pile of empty beer bottles, a broken tricycle, a spade, several earthenware pots, a dented pressure cooker and piles of yellowed paper.

When he returned gingerly to the shed, he saw the snake, a full-grown cobra, had slithered out of its hiding spot and was standing with its hood up, threatening to strike. Bhaubaab stood at a safe distance, with a long stick in one hand and the flashlight in the other, calmly staring at it. Lakshmi handed him the things he had brought and stepped back.

"Should I call the others?"

"Shhh…" Bhaubaab said, handing him the flashlight.

Lakshmi took it and pointed the beam at the snake. The S-shaped shadow dancing on the wall behind the snake, whose scales shone like sequins, made the whole scene more dramatic than the simple man–animal conflict that it was. Bhaubaab struck the ground near the snake with the stick, and it lunged at it once, then quickly withdrew. When he struck again, closer, it dropped to the ground and slithered past the stick into the pile of coconuts so quickly that Lakshmi was startled into jumping and hitting his head on a low end of the sloping roof beam.

Bhaubaab tied the empty sack to one end of the two-foot-long pipe. "Get back," he said to Lakshmi, and slowly began dismantling the coconut fort. The snake was hissing from its hiding place. Bhaubaab was prodding the pile with the stick, when it suddenly shot out and struck at his arm. He managed to pull back just in time and the snake fell to the floor and tried slithering back into the coconuts. Bhaubaab prevented it by putting the stick in its path. The dissuaded snake went into another corner. It had been hissing continuously all along and was now out of breath. "Poor thing," Bhaubaab muttered as the snake panted like a dog, the spectacle on its hood expanding and contracting to the rhythm of its tortured breath. Lakshmi was drinking it all in keenly. Bhaubaab was entirely focused on the cobra. He grabbed a couple of gunny sacks and threw them on the coconuts, blocking the snake's path back into the gaps in the pile. He placed the gunny bag tied to the pipe along the wall in front of the snake and began tapping on the floor behind the reptile. The snake slithered into the bag through the pipe. Within a second of this, Bhaubaab placed the stick across the sack to prevent the snake from biting him through the cloth and grabbed hold of the mouth of the sack. He removed the pipe and expertly tied up the sack with one hand while using the other to press the stick against it to hold the snake within at bay. He then stuck a hook at the mouth of the sack. Finally, he slung the bag on the end of his stick and carried it out of the shed, holding the bag away from his body. Lakshmi, who had stood gaping at him through all these manoeuvres, jumped out of his way. Bhaubaab squatted down to grab another bag, while holding up the bag with the snake in it to keep it from touching the ground. With Lakshmi's help, he opened the second bag and put the first one into it, reinforcing the snake's trap. "Bring your scooter around, Lakshmi," he said. Lakshmi ran home and rode back to Bhaubaab's on his scooter.

Together, they rode to a thickly wooded area a few kilometres away, with Bhaubaab carefully holding the stick with the snake bag at its end away from their bodies. When they got there, he quickly removed the sack with the snake from the outer one, untied its mouth and put it on the ground, before moving away to a safe distance. He then prodded the sack with a stick. The snake cautiously slithered out, staying close to the sack for a moment. It flicked its tongue around and, when it established the absence of threat, it moved off into the foliage and was lost to the eye.

That evening, over beer and salted cashews, Bhaubaab explained the science and craft of snake-catching to Lakshmi, who hung on to his every word.

"I always wanted to catch an Indian cobra. I heard they are among the easiest venomous snakes to catch. And it was so," he said.

"That was not a king cobra?"

"Of course not. Don't be silly. Didn't you see the spectacle mark on it? Anyway, unlike some African species, these aren't spitting cobras, which makes catching them a lot less risky. Also, unlike vipers, Indian cobras tend to mock strike without actually biting, just to warn you off – that gives you some leeway. The trick is to stay calm. If you panic, you may get jumpy and threaten the snake more – which is already defensive and edgy – and cause it to strike."

"Oh."

"Also, cobra fangs are short, as they are attached to the jaw, as opposed to the much longer ones in vipers that are attached to a hinge and can be folded back up when its mouth is closed. So, some bites may be dry. The venom is a neurotoxin. It's certainly fatal, but, if treated in time, the chances of tissue damage are fewer. That's usually the case with hemotoxin snakebites."

Lakshmi nodded, pretending to understand. "What was that you did with the pipe and the bag?"

"Oh, that's simple. Basically, when threatened, snakes seek a dark crevice or a hole to hide in. The trick is to cover up all such places and make sure your contraption is the only hiding place available. As soon as it enters the bag, place a hard object – a stick or a shoe – on the mouth of the bag to keep the snake from biting you through it. Tie up the mouth securely and quickly, and remember to keep the bag away from your body at all times. We must use a bag made of sturdy material, or at least put another one over it, just to make sure the snake is secure in it. A bag made of natural material like jute or cotton is what I prefer. And, of course, there should be no holes in it. Now, the most important thing: we must release the snake in the wild without delay, or all our efforts will be useless. It will suffocate and die in the bag. That has happened a couple of times with me," he said ruefully.

"How many have you caught?" Lakshmi was incredulous.

"Snakes in general? Many. Lost count. But this is my first Indian cobra. I started when I was quite young. Our servant, Erevu, taught me secretly, without my parents' knowledge. There were many snakes around where we lived. He had a great love for them and didn't want them killed. He was the one people called if a snake entered someone's home. I used to go as his assistant. But, one day, my brother found out and—" His voice caught.

"He told on you?"

"Not right away. He…well…he gave me a hard time over it," Bhaubaab said, looking away.

"What did he do?"

"Hmmm? It was all so long ago. Anyway, when my parents found out, they fired Erevu. But he had taught me enough by then. I caught a few on my own after that. The little wisdom he had passed on to me was more functional – how to tell different species apart, what a snake does when cornered, how to gauge its moves, etc. I learned more facts about them on my own, later. The UK is quite unexciting in the matter of snakes. Adders are the only venomous snakes there and you barely see any of those. All you get are grass snakes and slow worms – which are not even snakes but legless lizards!"

"Will you teach me how to catch snakes?" Lakshmi suddenly asked.

"It isn't exactly a hobby idea, you know?"

"No. I want to learn…" Lakshmi hesitated. "I want to…I want to be like you."

Bhaubaab looked at him keenly before smiling. He regaled him with stories of snakes until he tired. Lakshmi stayed over that night.

"Where do you think that snake went after we released it?" Lakshmi asked over coffee the next morning.

"You are still thinking about it? Well, I hope it found a nice safe place in the forest, or it may come back. Cobras are territorial. Quite like dogs. They like to be in their own areas."

"You mean they don't go barking up the wrong tree? Hehe…"

"It's an evolved trait. Not a dogma." Bhaubaab smiled at him fondly. Lakshmi looked delighted.

*

Everyone knew it had been a foolhardy act – an entirely avoidable accident. But it's always easier on the mind if there is an actual person to blame. Bhaubaab had been away for a few days when the unfortunate incident occurred, but it was he who was accused of putting ideas as stupid as "rescuing" snakes in the young, vulnerable lad's head. He was unaware of all the gossip that had gone on while he was away. He went to visit Lakshmi as soon as he heard about the amputation.

Lakshmi's parents' politeness barely hid their frigid feelings for him, and they were staunchly reticent when asked about the details of the incident. They served him milky tea, which he gulped down, not wanting to offend them by refusing it. But when he asked to see Lakshmi, they claimed he was asleep. Bhaubaab was taken aback by this. That's when it began to dawn on him that he was being held responsible for the unfortunate incident. It was from the *poder* that he got the whole story. Bhaubaab's was among the last houses in his beat, and the *pau* and *poies* in the enormous wicker basket covered in blue plastic were nearly sold out. The little Oriya man was only too happy to get a *gutka* break when Bhaubaab broached the topic of Lakshmi's snakebite incident. He leaned his bicycle on the wall and, with a fresh grab of *gutka* in his mouth, launched into the story.

Lakshmi had started walking confidently through the overgrowth that lay between the two houses instead of taking the paved detour like before. He had been spouting a whole lot of nonsense about the snake being man's cohabiter on the earth and snakes only attacking in self-defence and not wanting to hurt humans and some such. That day, when he saw a cobra there, instead of gathering men to pound it to a pulp, he had run home and got a pipe and a sack and had excitedly tried catching it. He had said something about the same cobra coming back. It was late evening. Light was fading and he had messed the whole thing up. The cobra had struck and had bitten him on his left thumb. Hearing his screams, neighbours rushed to his aid. They tied a tourniquet on his arm and—

"That is the *one* thing you are *not* supposed to do!" Bhaubaab hissed through clenched teeth.

Well, they rushed him to the primary healthcare centre, where he was administered the antivenom that saved his life. But his thumb had gone black, and the skin was peeling off. They took him to a private hospital in Madgaon, where they said they had no choice but to amputate his thumb.

"What did the snake look like?"

The *poder* knew that too. Although not an eyewitness, he had drunk in every detail of the incident. It was pretty much all anyone had spoken about the past few days. It was brown and around five feet long and had black ring-like patterns all over its body. Snout like a dog too. The *poder* had a theory about what had gone wrong, of course, just like everyone else in the village. The cobra had not raised its hood in warning, so Lakshmi had not expected it to strike—

"Bollocks! That's not a cobra. That's a bloody Russell's viper! The venom is hemotoxin. That wanker cannot tell a rat snake from a rat's arse. Why did I ever talk to him about rescuing snakes? Oh, the fucking knobhead!" Bhaubaab yelled.

The *poder* was unperturbed at this outburst. He spat out a red stream and asked Bhaubaab if he had learned his dark art from African "tribals".

*

Bhaubaab waited sorrowfully for Lakshmi to get better and visit him. He looked out the back window towards Lakshmi's house every now and then to catch any sign of activity. But the house was dumb in its inertial stupor.

Word had got around that the *Afrikar baab* did black magic and lit snake-oil lamps and danced around wearing face paint on new-moon nights. While Goan life itself was fecund with pagan lore and practices which had seamlessly integrated with Lusitanian Catholicism, and each village, church, chapel had its own haul of supernatural and paranormal stories, Africa was still far away and very, very dark. What came from that continent was nowhere close to Goa's own garden-variety occult, and people feared strangeness.

Lakshmi's sister-in-law had begun walking the extra distance to dump her baby's used diapers in the low ground following the hedge before Bhaubaab's house, instead of in the stream on the other side of their house. Hungry pigs pulled the diapers apart, dragging them over the tar road, leaving shit-covered lumps of cotton all over the place. The water buffalos that walked that route back to the village from their grazing grounds dropped their dung on the cotton, and the reinforced paste was pressed further into the tar by the sand-mining trucks that rolled over it every day. As the road in front of his house turned foul-smelling and lumpy, Bhaubaab grew more morose. Although loneliness wasn't new to him, he liked his solitude to be a choice rather than an imposition. And he was deeply injured by the thought that the people in this place he was hoping to make a home of were angry with him for risking the life and thumb of a young man.

His only consolation was his beloved baobab tree, which he gazed at for extended lengths of time. It was on one such evening when he stood under the baobab, looking vacantly into space, that he got a call on his mobile phone from an unknown number.

"Hello?"

"Er…Tio Caje?" said a young female voice on the other end of the line.

*

After a brief jaunt through central Karnataka, writing about the ancient baobab trees of Savanur, and a quick visit to Hampi for a joint, a schnitzel and to watch the Tungabhadra flow, Sylvia had caught the Amaravati Express to Goa to join her old school friends for a reunion. She hadn't met these three women since they finished school and they had barely been in touch in the past decade. It wasn't as if they had been particularly close back in school, but there had been no bad blood between them either, and Sylvia was curious to see how they had all turned out. One of them had studied hotel management at some top college or other, another one had a degree in physiotherapy, but the current highlight was that she was all set to head to Dubai by the end of the year with her IIM graduate of a soon-to-be husband. The third had just finished her MBA in HR management and was "placed" in a multinational corporation in Gurgaon – a top one too. Sylvia had already forgotten which of them was what.

They arrived by air an hour before her and brought the cab to the tiny Vasco da Gama railway station to pick her up. There was much hugging and squealing for joy, and congratulating each other over their accomplishments, before they piled into the cab and headed north to Anjuna, where they were booked in a resort. As the cab got stuck in traffic on the Zuari Bridge, Rashmi, who was sitting in the front by the driver, turned around and spoke to Sylvia. "Dude, did you know your state was in such a state?"

Everyone laughed at the pun, but Sylvia responded with a bored look. "Hardly *my* state. Just because I'm a Pereira doesn't make Goa my state."

"Your family is not from Goa? Mangalore, then?" Archana, the freshly minted hotel-management graduate asked.

"My father traces his roots to Goa. Aldona, I think. He grew up in Africa and the UK though, so there has been no connection with Goa since his generation. I have lived all my life in Bangalore, anyway. I am just a visitor here, like the rest of you."

31

The conversation veered to the "huge rock" on Tina's finger and how she met the man she was engaged to marry. Sylvia stared out of the window as, amid gasps and "ohmigods", Tina narrated the whole story, sparing no detail. It was only when they were stuck again, this time on the Mandovi Bridge, that they realised Sylvia had been quiet all along. "So? Writing and all, uh?" Rashmi said. "Not bad, dude. I'm so glad you are following your heart. It's real brave of you, you know? My parents would never allow me to do something like that. With my package, one break year would mean a huge dent in my earnings. Takes guts to do what you are doing." Everyone agreed Sylvia was indeed the most courageous of the lot, and then went back to discussing Tina's upcoming "dream wedding".

After two days of swimming in the sea, followed by drinking and dancing to loud Bollywood music at night, Sylvia wanted a break from the RATS, as they were calling themselves by then. She excused herself from the dolphin-spotting boat ride with DJ music that afternoon, to be alone. As she ate a lunch of batter-fried calamari and sautéed vegetables, she read the dramatic memoir of a political family of a dystopian South Asian country, written by its scholar member of the current generation. She continued reading over a couple of beers and took a long nap after finishing the book. She woke up feeling refreshed and immensely superior. She texted her friends that she wouldn't make it to the party that evening and went for a swim in the pool of the Brine and Breeze.

The water was on the chilly side, but she had the pool to herself. She did about ten vigorous laps to work the beer out of her system, before turning around to float on her back. Encased between the blueness of the sky above and the water below her, she was enjoying the feeling of being all alone in the world when something small and light hit her on her breast. She jerked her head to see a cigarette butt floating in the water. She lifted her head further to see the curtains of a room on the first floor being quickly pulled shut. Her illusion rudely shattered, she swam to the ladder and hauled herself out. She went to the restroom by the pool to change out of her swimsuit. As she bent her knees to hover over the bowl to urinate, something on the door caught her eye.

Old issues of the *oHeraldo* were hung on a string, for wrapping soiled panty liners and tampons before dumping them in the rubbish-bin. The article that had grabbed her attention was titled *Goa's Prodigal Son is Charmed by Snakes*, and featured the picture of a middle-aged man holding a sack which apparently contained a snake. The subheading read *Cajetan Pereira returns from Africa to rescue Goa's snakes*. Sylvia quickly wrapped a bathrobe around herself and grabbed the paper before stepping out of the restroom. She sat on a poolside chair and read the article carefully. It took an hour of calling friends in the press and waiting for them to call other people and return her call before she got his number. It took her another half hour to draw up the courage to call.

"Hello?" His deep voice sounded curious.

"Er…Tio Caje?"

"What?"

"Um…sorry. Is this Mr Cajetan Pereira?"

"Yes. Who is this?"

"My name is Sylvia. Sylvia Pereira. I think I'm your niece."

Her friends were surprised when she told them she wanted to cut short her holiday with them to visit her uncle.

"But didn't you say you had no family here?"

"I thought I didn't, but I found out I do," she said simply.

They expressed their dismay that she was leaving so soon; after all, they had only just become RATS together. They extracted promises to stay in touch and to meet again at Tina's destination wedding, and took many group selfies before sending her off with hugs.

He had given her an address and precise directions. She was to take the Kadamba shuttle from Panjim to Madgaon and then hire a motorcycle-pilot from there, and not pay more than 150 rupees for the ride. As soon as she got on the bus, she put her backpack down, pulled her phone out and exited the RATS WhatsApp group.

*

Bhaubaab had been restless all day. He paced his long porch. He walked up to the baobab and jumped into its enclosure, over the fence, and touched its trunk. He leaned on it and stood staring blankly into space. He jumped back out and ran home to begin pacing again. He could not define his feelings. They were a potpourri of everything possible in the spectrum of human emotions. His brother Anton – Antonio – was five years older than him. He had been his role model, his hero for the longest time. Bhaubaab had tried to be like him, to imitate his every word and action. Anton had been their parents' favourite. Born after many candles were lit to Our Lady of Immaculate Conception, their golden boy could do no wrong.

Having had to overcome the early years of infertility with meditation and prayer, the second son's unpremeditated birth had not been reason for particular excitement. He was loved instinctively, but attention wasn't lavished on him like it was on the made-to-order Anton. Bhaubaab hadn't minded that at all.

In fact, he was happy that his idol was indeed everyone's darling. Which is why what happened later had been so devastating. Unlike lesser injuries, one never heals from betrayals. The most one can do, after years of striving to forget, is become cynical. While their parents had been as staunchly devout in their faith practices as only expats can be, Bhaubaab had accepted his non-believing brother's lack of faith. He had joined in the laughter and the mockery of religion just to please Anton at first, learning to articulate his rationality to himself later. But neither of them outwardly defied their parents. They went along respectfully with the Bible classes, Communion, confession, novenas, Lent and everything that was asked of them, without so much as rolling their eyes in protest. They did not want to be rebels. As long as they could be whoever they wished to be in the privacy of their own minds, it didn't matter. Or so Bhaubaab thought.

Once, when Bhaubaab must have been around twelve, the new priest, a Goan man who had arrived recently from Lisbon, had been invited over by his parents to bless their home. After the blessings had been bestowed and *doce de grao* and tea had been partaken of, the priest sat on the large armchair in the living room, beaming at the boys who had been washed and dressed in stiffly starched shirts and presented before him for his grace and advice.

"You are lucky to have parents like yours. They are very good people. Good Goans. Tell me, boys, what have you learned from them?"

Bhaubaab was offended by this patronising question. He bowed his head and shuffled, trying not to show his irritation. He looked uncomfortably at Anton for support. But, instead of sharing his chagrin, Anton met the priest's gaze with great humility and responded in a soft voice, "Charity, Father. We have learned the value of charity from our parents. They are very giving people, and we try to emulate that in everything we do. If we manage to achieve a quarter of their charitable nature in this lifetime, we would consider ourselves to be good Christians."

Bhaubaab remembered how impressed the priest had been and how his parents' eyes had welled up. When they were busy accepting the priest's congratulations at having such a wonderful son, Anton had looked at Bhaubaab and winked. Bhaubaab had been wonderstruck by his brother's impudence. If anything, it should have served as a warning of his self-serving duplicity. But he hadn't realised that. And so, he was hurt beyond belief when, rather than assure him of his support, Anton had smirked and said, "Poof," when he confided in him his feelings for Erevu.

"Don't tell Mama," Bhaubaab had pleaded with him, suddenly unsure.

Anton had only sneered and said, "We'll see."

The torture had been steady and sadistic. Anton did not blackmail Bhaubaab into doing his chores for him, as one may have imagined. Instead, he stretched him over a greater number of smaller sins, slowly testing the limits of his mental capacity for punishment. That avocado pit hurled at the priest's head was blamed on Bhaubaab. As he opened his mouth to deny it vehemently when his parents questioned him about it, Bhaubaab caught the smug look on Anton's face and simply hung his head in passive acceptance of the allegation. The first time, his parents had been kind in their admonishing of his rascally act – they hugged him and explained why it was wrong and why they would like him not to repeat it, and that the forgiving Lord would give him a second chance.

"Monkey lover," Anton whispered as soon as his parents left him alone to mull over the wrong of his actions.

They were less forgiving when Bhaubaab confessed to peeing on the potted plants by the chapel. He received a hard slap from his father that sent him reeling when he confessed to scratching out the image of male parts on a church pew with a penknife. He was whipped until welts stood out on his back and arms when a rude drawing involving the priest had been found in the charity box after Sunday Mass.

He sat sobbing in a corner when Anton came over to him. "Poor monkey lover. Poor, poor monkey lover. Did Pai hurt you a lot? Look at those puffy cheeks. Poofy cheeks. Why! You look like one of the piccaninnies you love so much!"

The pain and the humiliation shot to his head and Bhaubaab lunged at his brother and bit him hard on his cheek until he bled. His father rushed in, hearing the screams, and pulled him away. He proceeded to whip Bhaubaab more, without stopping to ask what had transpired. Bhaubaab couldn't take the injustice of it all any longer. He cried out that all the mischief that had happened so far had been Anton's doing. His father paused from the beating to look questioningly at Anton.

"Caje is a faggot," Anton yelled back, the redness of his streaming eyes matching the raw red of his bleeding cheek.

His father turned to look at Bhaubaab in dumbstruck revulsion. "Is that true?" he asked. Bhaubaab did not respond. His father flung down the belt with which he had been beating him and walked out in disgust.

*

Erevu was fired and Bhaubaab never heard from him again. The family made plans to leave Tanzania soon after. It took them a couple of years to wind up and find decent jobs in the UK.

It was a time when African colonies, newly independent from European rule, were establishing themselves as modern nation states. Indian families in the continent were steadily emigrating to the US, Canada and Europe, fearing backlash from the politically empowered black man, who they worried would be vengeful towards the brown man for having played second fiddle to the white man in oppressing and exploiting him in his own home. While the Pereira family's migration to the UK coincided with the general brown exodus from Africa, Bhaubaab's parents never let him forget that this heavy move had been necessitated by the shame he had brought upon them.

His accountant father and schoolteacher mother found jobs in London and bought a small apartment in Wembley with the money they got from selling their sprawling home in Dar es Salam. They began life afresh, feigning ignorance of Bhaubaab's "deviance", but it was too late – the family had irrevocably fallen apart. Anton and Bhaubaab no longer spoke to each other, and meals were such depressingly silent affairs that their mother stopped insisting the family eat together. Anton, who was already in his late teens, left home for college soon after. Bhaubaab continued to live with his parents for a while as they went through the motions of middle-class family life – working, cooking, eating, praying, watching TV and going to church – but the biting cold of their hearts underneath the thin veneer of normalcy was painful. Bhaubaab soon found work as a farmhand and left home to live in the country. His parents' protestations at his choice of career were only cursory and so was their welcome when he visited them on holidays. He eventually saved some money and earned a diploma in agriculture and got a managerial job with a company that sold heavy agricultural machinery.

As a last-ditch effort to please his parents, he had a platonic courtship and married a sweet-natured Catholic girl. The marriage was an affectionate one for the year it lasted. When she left over his inability to consummate it, she promised to remain friends. They lost touch soon after, and neither was surprised by it.

His parents had died of heart attacks within a year of each other. The last he had heard of Anton was that he had moved to India to work as the creative director of a large advertising agency and had married and settled down there. Now, nearly thirty years after losing touch with him, here was a young woman calling him on the phone, claiming to be his only brother's daughter.

*

He poured himself two more fingers of bourbon and waited. Lakshmi's amputation wound had healed and he had regained his strength; self-pity was all that was ailing him now. The unexpectedness of the arrival on his doorstep that afternoon of this young woman dressed in a black tank top and bottle-green chinos, wearing a large rucksack on her back, was the distraction he needed to snap out of it.

"Er...I'm looking for Mr Cajetan Pereira," she said.

"He lives in that house over there," Lakshmi said as he pointed out Bhaubaab's house.

"Oh, I'm sorry. The motorcycle-pilot dropped me here. How do I get there? I don't see a path through the undergrowth."

"It's on the other side. Let me show you. In fact, let me walk you there."

"No, no. I wouldn't dream of bothering—"

"It's no bother at all. Mr Pereira – Bhaubaab, as we call him here – is a dear friend. I have been meaning to visit him anyway."

*

One look at Sylvia removed all doubts from Bhaubaab's mind that she was indeed the daughter of his long-lost brother. The awkwardness of meeting her for the first time completely masked the awkwardness of meeting Lakshmi after the long, tragic gap, and he was quite relieved about it. Lakshmi looked at Bhaubaab with a mixture of contrition and sadness. Bhaubaab's warm smile put him immediately at ease. Bhaubaab's gaze shifted back to Sylvia, who was standing there wondering what to say or do.

"So, you are Anton's daughter." It was a statement rather than a question.

"Yes. And you are my uncle."

"Come in. You can put your bag down in that room. Where did you say you are coming from? Anjuna?"

"Yes. I was there with some friends, but I live in Bangalore."

"Does your father know you are meeting me?" he asked cautiously.

"No." A strange look came over Sylvia's face. "I haven't seen him in over twenty years now. I don't know where he is."

"What? You too? This seems to be a family tradition. What happened?"

"It's a long story."

"Isn't it always?"

Lakshmi stood by silently, watching the exchange. Having been Bhaubaab's only friend and confidant ever since he had arrived in these parts, Lakshmi sensed a shift in dynamics upon the arrival of a blood relative. They were family, and he was suddenly the outsider.

"Let's all sit down. How about a drink?" Bhaubaab suggested.

Sylvia didn't want one right away and said she needed a wash first. Bhaubaab went to show her the bathroom and came out to see Lakshmi heading towards the gate.

"Where are you off to? What about that drink?"

"I'll come back later," he called out.

"Come for dinner then."

Lakshmi nodded and left. But he didn't come back that evening.

Bhaubaab made chicken Xacuti and bought fresh *poies* from the *poder*. Alone with her uncle, Sylvia narrated the second half of Anton's story over dinner. Sylvia's mother, a fresh literature graduate, had been interning with the advertising agency in Bombay where Anton was the creative director, she began.

"Oh, I know how that goes," said Bhaubaab. "They met, fell in love, got married, had you, fell out of love and ended it. Is that it?"

Sylvia gave him a condescending smile.

"Why? Did I get it wrong?"

"No. But who says 'fell in love' anymore? You are so quaint."

"So, what do they say? Courted? Dated?"

"Never mind what they say. Let's get back to the story. My mother was young and impressionable. He was older, very well read and knowledgeable, and she found that attractive. He was a handsome man, moreover – he was quite popular with the ladies. She was awestruck that he gave her special attention. They began seeing each other. Her conservative Hindu family was against the match. She thought she was being strong and independent in eloping with him. He earned well and they were able to live comfortably. I was born a year into the marriage and was named after Plath – the only poet who 'spoke' to my mother, apparently. Things began unravelling soon after that. She realised he was not being faithful. He became violent when she questioned him about his affairs and beat her. Quite badly. I was a baby then and only know it from what my mother told me."

Bhaubaab was visibly distressed. "That bastard! Just how much cruelty was he capable of!" he muttered.

"Quite a bit, it turns out. Mama couldn't leave him. She could not go back to her parents, who were still angry with her for insulting them by marrying against their wishes. She had quit her job when she had me. She couldn't get another one right away because I was too young to be left alone."

Bhaubaab had tears in his eyes, but he did not say anything.

"It was soon after my fifth birthday that, after a particularly bad bout of beatings, Mama grabbed me and ran out in the middle of the night. We stayed with one of her former colleagues, who was surprised to hear that my father – the suave gentleman with the intelligent eyes, smart beard, charming smile and proper British accent – was a wife-beating monster. But she believed my mother's black eye and cut lip, and took her in.

"After about a month or so, my mother managed to contact one of her old college mates in Bangalore, who helped her get a teaching job in a fancy school there. I used to lock myself up in my room and obsessively thumb through my prized picture books during my parents' fights and mother's weeping. I was an early reader, and I guess that helped me somewhere. I sailed through the 'talent exam' for the same school and was granted admission on a full scholarship. Mama was relieved that, since we were on the same premises all day, she didn't have to feel that she was leaving me behind for a career."

"What happened to Anton?"

"We are not in touch." Sylvia paused before resuming. "Mama told me that he had tried contacting her a few times. At first, he wanted to apologise and to ask her to return, and when she wouldn't do his bidding, he threatened her with suicide. When she still wouldn't budge, he began sending her death threats. We slept with all our windows shut and the bedroom door firmly locked for the longest time, and Mama wouldn't allow me to go out, even to visit friends after school. That didn't bother me though, as all I wanted to do was stay home and read anyway. Then the threats eased up. As a high-profile advertising professional, he was in the news – in society pages of magazines, etc. – and we vaguely knew of his whereabouts. But he disappeared after a while. Good riddance."

"I'm so sorry for what my brother did to you and your mother, my dear. He is a horrible, horrible person. If only I'd known. I wouldn't have let you suffer like you did."

"We turned out okay. It doesn't bother me anymore. I read myself out of it all."

"I am curious. How did you know about me?"

"My father often mentioned you."

"Oh?"

"Every time I did something that annoyed him, he'd say I was just like you. You have always been a part of my life, you know? I remember the first time was when I was about three. He was beating Mama and I must have been upset. I flew at him and bit him hard on his hand. He screamed and flung me aside and yelled I was just like my Tio Caje." Sylvia didn't tell him her father had, in fact, said, "Just like your Tio Caje, the filthy faggot." Not that she had understood what it meant back then. "It was the way he mentioned you that made me feel he had hurt you too in some way and that we could be friends. I have always wanted to meet you."

Bhaubaab smiled sadly. "Well, neither of us gave up without a fight, did we?"

"We didn't give up at all."

Past midnight, when he got up to have a drink of water, Bhaubaab noticed the light was on in Sylvia's room. He peeped in to see why she was still up, but discovered that she was, in fact, fast asleep. He thought she must have fallen asleep reading, and switched the light off and went back to his room.

The next morning, as they sat drinking coffee on the *sopo*, Sylvia asked Bhaubaab if he had turned off the light in her room last night.

"Yes. Why? Should I not have?"

"No. It's fine. I was asleep anyway."

"What is it? Another Anton story?"

Sylvia told him. She had been scared of being alone in the dark as a child, and every night she would insist that her mother sit with her in her room until she fell asleep. One evening, she was particularly sleepy and began insisting that her mother leave her cleaning and take her to bed. Her father wouldn't hear of it and sternly asked her to go and sleep on her own.

"Just for five minutes, Daddy," she pleaded with him, but he wouldn't listen. Mama wanted to go in with her, but Daddy put his foot down and yelled at his wife for making a weakling of his child.

"Go in," he said sternly, "and lie down without making a fuss. Let your mother finish her work." She had asked if she could have the light on, but he hadn't allowed that either. "What are you scared of? Ghosts? What is a ghost? Hmm? Tell me. Tell me now!" She had whimpered that she didn't know. "See? It's nothing. You are *my* daughter. Mine! I will not accept cowardice in you. Now, go to bed!"

She had gone into the dark room, covering her mouth tightly with her hand so he wouldn't hear her cry. She had lain down on the bed while not moving her eyes from the door, through which she could see the lit dining room. Her father sat with one leg crossed over the other on the sofa, reading the paper, while Mama cleared the dinner table. Mama was looking back at Sylvia helplessly and there seemed an almost physical tunnel between their eyes that cut through the cavernous blackness around her, and she concentrated on it, trying not to blink and break the connection and let the dark flood in. Finally, after her father left the room, Mama rushed to her and hugged her. Sylvia sobbed silently into her mother's bosom before finally falling asleep. Mama had wept with her.

Bhaubaab dabbed at his eyes with his wrist. "What does your mother say about us meeting?" he asked after a long pause.

"She was sceptical. She didn't think anyone from my father's family could be a good person. I must call and correct her. To be honest, I wasn't sure about meeting you myself, but curiosity got the better of me when I saw that newspaper clipping. What could you do to hurt me anyway, I thought. I am perfectly capable of fighting back now," she said, and laughed. "I wasn't planning on staying over. I have surprised myself."

"I'm glad you did. Please stay for as long as you'd like. You are the only family I have."

That evening, Lakshmi joined them for dinner. He stayed back for a drink and a game of Scrabble. Since Bhaubaab and Sylvia had managed to fill in the gaps of each other's stories, and had had a combined catharsis of sorts, they were more relaxed with each other than they had been the previous day. They also welcomed Lakshmi's presence for the much-needed break from the poignancy of the past twenty-four hours.

After Sylvia's arrival, Lakshmi overcame his parents' reservations about his meeting Bhaubaab and began frequenting the house again. He and Sylvia became good friends. She was sorry to hear of his amputation, which he told her about only when they were out of Bhaubaab's hearing. Her sympathy helped him talk about his Bangalore experience. Speaking of the city where he had almost found fame, Lakshmi began to feel nostalgic.

Sylvia had not planned on staying when curiosity first brought her to Bhaubaab's. Then, relieved at how easily she could talk to him, she had thought of staying for a few days. She had spoken to her mother and helped her overcome her reservations too. It was her break year, and she had no concrete plans and was not bound by time to leave. In the second week of her stay there, she pulled out a kilo-heavy scented candle in a glass jar from her backpack and put it on the altar. It was pale blue, and the jar was shaped like a spherical pot.

"Smells lovely. What's it called?" Bhaubaab asked.

"'Fresh Linen'. Named by some poor copywriter who once dreamed of becoming a poet, clearly."

"Did you bring it for me? Thought you'd wait to see how you liked me before handing over the gift?"

"You give yourself too much credit, don't you?" Sylvia said with a mischievous smile. Their relationship had attained an affectionate playfulness. "It's my 'homing candle'. I light it in places I think of as home. And it was indeed bought for somebody, but I decided not to give it to them after all."

"I love your stories. Only wish they were happier ones."

"This one is! It is a funny one, in fact."

"Do tell."

"So, I was dating this interior designer when I was in college. He was older than I was by some years. He was rather proud of the fact that he had a young, college-going girlfriend and took me around for parties and things. One time, we were invited for dinner at the mansion of one of his clients and he was quite eager that I make a good impression on them. He had asked me to pick up a gift for them – 'Something tasteful. They spent a crore on the interior alone.' I bought this candle and made a bouquet of home-grown basil for them. Their house was huge, imposing and garish. Everything about it was glitzy, loud and expensive. I felt like I had stepped inside an oversized Greco-Roman-Caribbean crystal ball!"

"The description of it!" Bhaubaab laughed.

"Well, it was awful. The host gave us a tour. After showing us around what seemed like an expansive expensiveness, he stopped before a large, glass-covered print of a painting of a butterfly, with the legend 'Salvador Dali' written vertically in Comic Sans beside the image. 'Haha…rhinoceros,' I remarked hoping my reference to the famous scene where Dali obsesses with rhinos in the film *Midnight in Paris* would cover up my disgust. He gave me a curious look. 'No. It's a butterfly. It is by a Spanish painter called Salvador Dali. He is very famous,' he explained. Before I could respond, my boyfriend intervened with, 'Mr Shah, Sylvia has something for you.' I reached into my tote bag and pulled out the basil. 'Mr Shah, this is for you,' I said. 'Oh! Thank you so much. Is it organic?' he asked. 'Yes, of course,' I said. Later, in the car on our way back home, my boyfriend asked why I had not given them the candle. I told him

I had bought the candle for a home and not stupid houses like that. I felt something for that homeless blue candle. I couldn't have left it in that vulgar house. Since then, I have always carried it with me when I travel."

*

A month had passed when Sylvia asked Bhaubaab if she could write his memoirs.

"Why would anyone want to read my memoirs?"

"Because I will write it," she said, and smiled smugly.

"You do have a bit of your father in you," he responded.

"Can you promise never to say that again, please?"

Every afternoon, after their post-lunch siesta, they would carry two foldable chairs to the baobab. Settling under it, she would take notes while he recalled anecdotes about his life for her. They would sit there talking about Tanzania and Britain, and return home when it began to get dark. They would cook together and eat in companionable silence, each mulling over the stories of the day. Lakshmi would drop by after dinner for a drink and a chat. It was an easy routine.

Sylvia was reading aloud her previous day's writing to Bhaubaab one afternoon:

"It is that feeling. Looking at a baobab from my height of three feet or so, it felt like it engulfed the whole sky. Its top branches seemed like a roof on the world. My parents, my brother and I used to visit the baobab just outside Dar es Salam in our battered car. I don't remember anything about those trips except standing there and gazing up at the imposing tree – the sky cut, fissured by its clawing branches. Even in full leaf, it was never a canopy and offered a contrast with the light blueness of beyond. There was nothing above it, but the tree was the first marker of something tangible under that nothingness. My father told me the tree was more than a thousand years old. I don't know if that knowledge was given to me the first time I saw the tree or later, in the years that followed, on our regular visits. It is just part of my amorphous block of memory.

"The thousand years of the tree and its sky-length height were joined in an endlessness I revered. Space and time were indistinguishable in my mind. All it meant to me was it was big – big beyond my imagination. It felt like the most permanent thing in the world…in my life. We visited the tree regularly. I think I could see the top of its silhouette from our home in the gated Goan community in the city. I'm not sure. It might be something I have worked into my memory over the years. From afar, it wasn't as imposing as it was from below, but it felt like a symbol of itself – an idol of my fascination with it and it didn't diminish in its value. I looked at it through my parents' quarrels, poor school grades, bullying from peers, my brother's cruelty – and it was always there: solid; permanent; assuring."

"Edit out that part about my brother's cruelty."

"Why? We must be truthful."

"I don't want the whole truth. Just take it out."

"Okay," she said reluctantly, "but what do you think of the rest of it?"

"It's fine. A little too romantic, perhaps. And you make me sound like a tree-worshipping pagan," he said with a smile.

"Perhaps that's what you are."

"That's what we all are," Lakshmi joined in. Lost in her manuscript, they hadn't noticed him walk up to the tree.

"You, in fact, are a *kafir*," Bhaubaab replied sharply.

"Hey! What? What does that even mean?"

"A *kafir* is one who lacks faith. A pagan, on the other hand, is a person of deep faith. So much faith that he is incapable of containing it in one god. He's got to have many. A pagan sees gods in all of nature, all life forms. He respects the snake as much as he fears it. Doesn't stupidly get bitten by it." If Bhaubaab was joking, it wasn't apparent.

Lakshmi looked visibly hurt. He was about to turn around and head back when Sylvia tried to make light of it. "Lakshmi, wait! Don't forget, *kafirs* have the best food, *ya*…"

"Shut up!"

"No, really!" She ran behind him and put her arm around his shoulders. "Did you know Cafreal comes from *kafir*?"

"You're making that up."

"It's true. It's supposed to have originated in Africa…in Angola?" The last bit was directed at Bhaubaab.

"Mozambique," he corrected her.

"That's correct. It's an African recipe that the Portuguese brought to Goa. It's the food of the *kafir*. It was used as a pejorative once, but that's how it gets its name. It's African and Goan – much like your Bhaubaab here." She laughed.

By now, Bhaubaab was feeling sorry for the harshness of his earlier comment and wanted to make it up to Lakshmi. "Why don't we cook Cafreal for dinner tonight? Lakshmi, eat with us? Please?" Bhaubaab said.

They cooked together. Lakshmi washed and cleaned the coriander while Sylvia cut the chicken into curry-sized pieces. Sylvia noticed that Lakshmi was trying to ignore his missing thumb and work without it as efficiently as possible. Bhaubaab prepared to grind the masala. He had put the coriander, cinnamon, green chillies, bay leaf, cloves, cumin, ginger, garlic and a pinch of turmeric into the blender when he realised, they were out of coconut vinegar.

"Shall I replace it with lemon juice?" he asked.

"No, it has to be authentic," Sylvia said.

Lakshmi offered to bring some from his house. He returned in a few minutes with a glass of vinegar and a full bottle of Glenfiddich. His casino brother was visiting, and a rich client had gifted him the bottle. He had given it to Lakshmi for asking nicely.

The revelry of that evening was boisterous as they tossed back glass after glass of the single-malt whisky and ate potato wedges and Cafreal. Sylvia, happily tipsy, sitting with one leg folded up to her chin while the other dangled over the armchair, suddenly turned thoughtful. "I just realised how uncanny this whole string of events is. I was in central Karnataka, writing about the 1,800-year-old baobabs there, before coming to Goa. It was by sheer accident that I read about Tio Caje in the newspaper – that too a week-old paper. And where do I find him? Under another baobab!"

Lakshmi looked on, bedazzled by her thoughts, but Bhaubaab nodded knowingly.

"I'm not surprised," he said quietly. "That tree has powers beyond our comprehension."

But Sylvia was still preoccupied by the strange linkage she had only just made. "What are the odds? There are only a few such trees in the country. You can count them on the fingers of one hand," she said.

"Only four?" Lakshmi asked, goofily raising his thumbless hand. That broke the spell and they all burst into laughter. More whisky followed and they were hooting and singing before long. At one point, Bhaubaab put his arms around Sylvia and Lakshmi in a wide embrace and kissed them both on the cheek.

"This is wonderful. We are family. We are home. I'm the father, this is my daughter, and this lad here is a piece of my heart!" he exclaimed. Suddenly, the two younger people looked at each other and smiled uncomfortably. Bhaubaab, oblivious to their awkwardness, gulped down another shot. "I think I have had a drop too many," he said after that. "I better go lie down. You two, carry on…carry on…Tally-ho and all that sort of thing…Night!"

He staggered off to his room. Sylvia and Lakshmi sat exchanging drunkenly deep gazes with each other across the table. She put her glass down, reached over and slowly traced the outline of his face with her outstretched finger. He leaned over and kissed her on the lips. She flung her arms around his neck and clamped her mouth on his.

*

The sun had been up a while when Sylvia stirred, half asleep, in Lakshmi's arms the next morning. He hugged her closer. "I love you," he muttered, without opening his eyes.

Suddenly, Sylvia was more alert. "What did you just say?"

"I said I love you," he said, and smiled, opening his eyes.

"Why? What happened?" She sat bolt upright and looked out of the window. "I miss home," she said at length.

Lakshmi didn't understand, but before he could ask her to explain, she stood up and strode out of the room. Lakshmi waited for some time, puzzled at what had just transpired, before getting up to go after her. He ran into Bhaubaab at the door. Their eyes met briefly, but neither said anything. After a wordless moment, Lakshmi looked away. Almost immediately, he left for his house.

Later that morning, when Sylvia couldn't find Bhaubaab anywhere in the house, she went looking for him in the one place she knew he'd be. Bhaubaab stood with a lost look on his face under the baobab. She walked to his side and stood by him silently, looking at the same expanse of paddy crops as he.

"It's time I went home," she said, after some time.

"Is it?" he asked, without looking at her.

"Yes."

There was a long pause before he responded. "Stay, child. You are not like your father." He sounded resigned, however.

"I try not to be like him. I don't know how successful I am," she said, her eyes welling up. They hugged.

The taxi service was not very reliable there. Bhaubaab borrowed Lakshmi's scooter, which he no longer used since losing his thumb, and dropped Sylvia off at the Madgaon bus stand. He bought her a ticket for thirty-six rupees for the shuttle to Vasco. She would get off at the airport junction and take a flight to Bangalore.

"Oh, wait," she said, before he turned around to leave. She reached into her bag and pulled out her homing candle. "Please give this to Lakshmi."

Part II

EGGSHELLS

It was raining when the boy of four came, holding a folding umbrella with broken spokes in one hand and six rupees in two-rupee coins in the other, leaving neither hand free to rub the sleep off his eyes. His low-ranking policeman father had returned home at ten from *dooti* and there was nothing to eat at home.

Five rupees each for intact eggs, three for cracked ones – you cannot boil them, but the omelettes give nothing of their brokenness away, the board read.

"There are no cracked eggs today," said the egg seller's wife. She looked like someone who, having grown up before her time, was now wanting to look her age. She had been roused from deep sleep but walking on eggshells, to not wake her sleeping husband, had left her wide awake. She examined the money in the boy's hands.

"You will get one egg for this and keep a rupee."

"Then please crack them, *akka*. I must have two. *Abbu* is very hungry."

She thought for a minute before handing him two eggs wrapped in an old newspaper.

"Don't tell anyone they weren't broken." She grinned wide at the boy, like a child whose first milk teeth had just fallen. She shut the door softly after him and walked on eggshells back to her sleeping husband.

BHAGIRATI

Where she came from, bribes were called *kushi* – joy – a term that ironed out the ignominy of the act and the plosive in the first syllable of the original word, rendering it local and easy. They had given a kushi of 500 rupees to the clerks of the marriage registrar to have their turn pushed up the queue on their wedding day. The wedding was worth thirty rupees on the cash memo. But it was a happy occasion, and they hadn't minded sharing their joy. There were three witnesses: the groom's father, the bride's room-mate and the lifeguard at the swimming pool where they had met. Kushi had continued into their lives as they sought answers and assurances to metaphysical bewilderments in each other's company, which she refused to call love. He did not mind the lack of verbal articulation of the feeling, as long as he felt it. That was before she heard the voice. Then they buried a pet together.

Bud Jackson was the dead man the school was named after. The American was visiting her village when he had fallen off a buffalo cart and died, long before she was born. What the white man was doing in that dusty, remote place was anybody's guess. His people, who had come to bury him, donated a sum of money and his portrait to the local merchants who ran a school. They put the money in their cotton mill and hung the portrait on a wall and changed the name of the school from Chimnabai Ghorpade Vidyamandir to Bud Memorial School. And, just like that, it became a "convent" overnight.

She decided he was "white-trash evangelical". This thought came to her long after she had rid herself of the school and its influence, of course. She wouldn't learn of the term "white trash" until she had read *Gone with the Wind* in college. "Evangelical" was from when someone at work said that her neighbour's aunt had been healed of her cancer by a man in a white suit. She learned to put the two together when politics in Bud Jackson's country took an unexpected turn (although some psephologists and media pundits argued it wasn't unexpected at all). The term somehow seemed to fit him. Not much was known of him by the teachers, and certainly not by the students, to whom he was nothing more than the *phorener* in the picture hanging on the wall behind the headmaster's desk. The headmaster's office was out of bounds and only the occasional truant child got to see its insides. Stick in hand, the stern headmaster would deliver his standard line: "Did Gandhi-*ji* fight the whites for freedom only for you to behave like this? You'll never grow up to go to America if you continue this way!"

At one point, America was a place she, too, aspired to go to. She saw herself wearing polka-dotted dresses, eating apple pies, making snowmen and living the Archie Comics life. Then, everyone started going there as IT professionals (how many white-trash evangelicals had to be dead and buried in India to facilitate this mass migration, she wondered), and she lost interest. She did go to an engineering college, all the same. Everyone did. There was nothing else to do.

He was fascinated by ferns, the extant variety of Jurassic plants that had survived the earth as it blew hot and cold, doing away with most of its contemporary animal species. They grew on the moist laterite walls of the university campus that was his home. The walls had long lost their original brown-orange

hue due to generations of moss covers that shone a light green
at the beginning of the rains and soon turned darker and duller
– which was most of the year – and dried to varying shades of
grey-brown during the brief dry spell. Ferns sprung out from
the cracks and holes in the pockmarked rock, like the occasional
thicker tufts in his father's mossy beard that served to soften his
sharp angular features. His father was a tall, square-shouldered
man of few words, with deep-set eyes that peered absently from
behind thick-rimmed glasses. When he smiled, his eyes popped
back in further, leaving endearing crow's feet around their
corners. He loved his father. And he loved the ferns.

His father had had many female admirers, who showed their
admiration in various ways, beginning soon after the proper
mourning period following his mother's death in a car accident.
Santosh was a baby when it happened, and he remembered
nothing of it. His mother was simply a smiling portrait on his
father's desk – and a whispered sympathy from strangers. He
had grown used to the steady flow of admiration directed at
his father, however. Some colleague or friend of his father's was
perpetually in the house, taking the fresh laundry out of the
dryer, bringing the "boys" a home-cooked meal, fawning over
him as he did his homework – all the while making sure his
father noticed.

Dr Prajapati – Pati to his friends and admirers, *Pati-pa*
to Santosh – accepted the admiration without comment,
neither encouraging nor dismissing their ministrations. Many
stayed over at the house – sometimes for weeks – but they all
eventually fell away, bored by his complacency, making way for
others. Then Santosh went to college, away from the lovely
fern-filled campus, to take his love for ferns to an academic
level at a university in the hot and dry next-door state. That he

had not followed in the footsteps of his father, the renowned professor of computer science, who belonged to a generation where engineers were people of science, was of more concern to others than to his father. You are throwing away your future, they warned him. He smiled, trying unconsciously to resemble his father, and did not comment. It was during a visit home that he met Bhagirati, his father's student.

Dr Pati's was the only course she did well in, while scraping through the others mostly because of her chronic indifference. She would go to his house after classes to discuss the subject. Unlike the other teachers, he never spoke to her about exams or the "job market". Instead, their conversations about computer science always wandered into topics such as set theory, event philosophy, or poetry. She would listen to him intently, and consciously avoid looking into his face. She wouldn't speak except to ask the occasional question. They sat in wicker chairs in his book-filled study until it got dark and they realised no one had bothered to turn the lights on. Then Dr Pati would clear his throat and awkwardly suggest tea and she would offer to make it herself. After they had drunk the tea in silence, she would shuffle up her things, smile at his feet and leave. It wouldn't be until she had turned the corner that she would relax and allow herself a sigh. He would stand on the balcony looking after her, smiling into his beard.

"You must meet my son," he said to her when she visited next. They had spent their time discussing Thomas Kuhn's idea of the "paradigm shift" in the history of science. "An important notion, before the corporates hijacked it," he said as she smiled demurely. She was gathering her books to leave when her teacher mentioned his son.

"Sure," she said non-committally.

"You will like him." He thought he saw a shadow of hurt pass on her face.

"Okay," she said quickly, smiling at his knees before stumbling out.

"Join that swimming pool outside the campus," Pati-pa said to Santosh when he came home. "It has longer laps." Santosh felt his father was a little more distracted than usual, but made no comment about it.

"Okay," he said simply.

He found Bhagirati staring in dismay at the notice on the gate of the swimming pool. He went up close to read it himself.

"They could have told us earlier that it would be closed for maintenance today," she said absently.

"Yeah," he said.

She turned around and looked at him. "You must be Dr Pati's son."

"How did you know?"

"You have, er…his eyes," she said, displaying keen knowledge for someone who put a great deal of effort into avoiding looking at her professor's face.

"You come here regularly?" he asked, to change the subject.

"I only just joined the pool. My father recommended it."

Santosh thought he saw a strange expression flit across her face.

"The pool on campus has weird timings. They only let women in at three in the afternoon – when men aren't around."

"When men don't want to be around," he said. "Giving 'x' is in fact an excuse to keep '100-x'."

"What?"

"Reservation."

"Oh." She looked at him again, more keenly now.

He wore shorts and a nondescript T-shirt and had a towel slung around his neck. She was wearing ash-coloured, calf-length sweatpants and a peach T-shirt that read, *You Winsome, You Lissom* in calligraphy, and she was clutching a shopping bag with what seemed like a swimming costume in it.

She told him about how she had discovered masturbation at the age of six while sitting astride her short-wheeled bicycle – the kind with the foot-long seat that curved up at the back and had a long, metallic, inverted "U" as a backrest, that was all the rage when she was growing up. The bike was at rest and, as she adjusted to balance herself better, something had felt strange and good. She had kept repeating the slight movement until she thought she'd had an epiphany. Only, she hadn't known the word then. No matter, she was still convinced she was in touch with a higher being.

"Sex and religion! Another time and another continent, you would have given Dora and Anna O a run for their money," he teased her.

She enjoyed that their jokes were esoteric. He told her that he never missed his mother and that he had lost his virginity to a woman fifteen years his senior. She nodded solemnly.

In the next few months, the usual performance of a relationship followed – sharing books, music, films, food, alcohol, sex, fights – before they decided they wouldn't have children. Overpopulation, depleting resources, climate change, hereditary diseases, the environment, increasing fundamentalism, xenophobia, nationalism and wars – the reasons they agreed on unanimously sounded like they were straight out of the anti-natalism discourse. She feared the pain of childbirth, she added, and hoped that the combination of justifications somehow made it more original. She had told her parents not to come for the wedding, as she did not want to give it undue importance. Father had fumed and wept. Mother had accepted it without question, like she did most things in life. Santosh's father had hugged her during their 530-rupee "joy" and it had felt divine. She had taken to calling him Pati-pa since she started dating Santosh, and had come to feel at ease looking him in the face when she spoke to him. She was more relaxed in his presence as his daughter-in-law than she had been as his admiring student. She would catch herself looking into the distance and smiling, sometimes.

Pati-pa refused to move in with them in spite of all their insisting. "I like my solitude," he said. Two months into their marriage, he surprised the newlyweds by going on a trek into the Sholas with some of his more adventurous students – something that the non-athletic, academic old man had never previously displayed an inclination for. There, while trying to cross a stream, he slipped on a mossy patch and hit his head hard on a rock. He never came out of his coma, and Santosh asked the doctor to pull the plug on the twentieth day.

*

It was the night after Mia died that they made love with a passion that seemed to have vanished since the early months of their courtship. Mia had always been a little stupid, and Santosh had suggested they keep her indoors at all times. Bhagirati had protested that it would be stifling for her. Moreover, cleaning cat litter wasn't a pleasant thought, so Santosh had given in. They'd had to rescue her out of sticky situations often – a window ledge on the fourth floor of the building, a water-filled ditch in a construction site next door, a wedge in a tall tree – since they had got her home as a scraggy little kitten from the shelter.

Although it was tacitly known that one day they may not reach her in time, they were still stunned and grieved when they found her dead under a tree, her bright calico fur bruised and matted with blood around the neck. They had placed her stiff body into a basket and brought her home and buried her in the backyard. He had dug the grave with a pickaxe, while she shovelled out the dirt.

Later that evening, as they sat silently across from one another at the table, Santosh doubled up and started crying violently, without warning. His strong, square shoulders shook as he leaned his face into his long bony hands, tears streaming down through his fingers. For someone who had always been stolid and stoic through a life marked by the death of a loved one, this strange, childlike reaction seemed very much out of character. Bhagirati walked over to him and held him in her arms, and he held her back gratefully.

Santosh worked as an assistant professor in the department of botany at a reputable university – a job that fitted him so well that it was hard to imagine he had ever been without it. With it came a high-ceilinged house with red terracotta flooring and a large, leafy backyard. Although there were no ferns here, it felt like home.

Bhagirati, on the other hand, lost three jobs in a row. She had decided not to use her engineering degree – which she hadn't cared for, to begin with – to get employment. Instead, she had taken her amateur environmentalism, in all earnestness, to an NGO that worked with access to safe water in drought-prone areas, and they had given her a job as junior project associate. The only non-obscure part in her job title was the one that entitled her to lesser pay. Her idealism kept her going through the most menial of tasks expected of her – sending out invites to high-profile guests for conferences, picking them up from the airport, staying back after the talk to pack up the projector and mics – and it was idealism that made her quit when she was asked to arrange for crates of mineral-water bottles for the evaluators who were going to the villages for a field visit.

She then joined the communications team of an NGO that worked with women and children. It went well initially, and she became good friends with one of her teammates who was about the same age. While she was glad of the friendship, Bhagirati was secretly resentful of her colleague's carefreeness – a fact she kept successfully hidden. She was equally fascinated and jealous. One of the reasons for it was that, unlike herself, her colleague had studied the humanities in college. "These Sandra-from-Bandra types are so lucky; they get to study language and literature and not get shoved into shitty professional courses," she said to Santosh, trying to sound light-hearted. Another reason for her envy was that, while her own shift in career had been hard won, her colleague called this her "day job" and didn't take it too seriously. Bhagirati was unfamiliar with this breezy attitude towards life. She, too, like her colleague and friend, wanted to care about people and causes with a detached objectivity, but didn't quite know how. When the communications team was thrown a "thesaurus party" to celebrate the funding it had won for a project from three different organisations for the same project, Sylvia decided she had spent enough time there and needed to quit and go off to do her own thing. Bhagirati quit along with her, with a comparably higher show of self-righteousness.

Santosh, who had shown some amusement when she left the first job, was a little more concerned after she quit the second one. "Perhaps you should do some research before taking up another job," he said. The third one, with a project that was lobbying to make rainwater harvesting legally mandatory for all new constructions throughout the state, did not have too big a gap between vision and practice, and she was happy to be a part of the team that was crowd-sourcing data. But when the lake started frothing over and killing all the fish, she knew it was time.

They had sent her home in a cab when she had physically attacked a colleague for immersing a Ganesh idol in her neighbourhood pond. The colleague hadn't pressed charges, but her boss insisted that Bhagirati take some time off work. It was around then that she had started talking about wanting a baby. Santosh had taken her to the counselling centre on the campus that was set up following a spate of student suicides. The counsellor suggested rest and distraction, along with vitamin supplements. After a fortnight, Bhagirati returned to work.

Three uneventful months followed. Then, one day, she forgot to come out of the swimming pool. The campus pool lifeguard, who knew her to be an excellent swimmer, had left her the keys to lock up after her swim – she usually went towards the end of the day, long after the students had left the pool. When she wasn't back by dinner time, Santosh went looking for her. He found her floating on her back at the shallow end of the pool. The lights were off, and he had walked in expecting the worst, since the gate was open. Her eyebrow stud caught the light from the torch and glinted.

She wasn't too badly off physically, apart from her hands and feet, which had turned soft and wrinkly white, and a cold that lasted a week. This time, they went beyond the campus to seek help. The psychiatrist at the colonial-looking establishment with the gentle white walls and pastel green borders had refused to label it. "It's easy to categorise and classify and be done with it. It can be stigmatising – a burden to carry all your life. I think we can make a breakthrough by mapping the logic that governs the alternative reality she slips into. Plus, it isn't as bad as you think. I'm sure CBT would be effective," he said in a soft and reassuring voice.

Bhagirati stopped going into work. She attended therapy twice a week and it seemed to be doing her good. She also joined a yoga course and practised diligently. She took an interest in cooking and was constantly experimenting with cuisines and recipes. She grew her own vegetables in the backyard, always struggling to keep Mia from digging up her carrots. She hosted small parties for Santosh's students, offering them non-vegetarian snacks and joking that they probably didn't like to eat their subject. She did mumble about having babies from time to time, but Santosh didn't give it much thought. After all, her general demeanour was more cheerful than ever. Then Mia died, and Bhagirati got pregnant.

*

When Santosh found out, he was angry, confused and scared. "But hadn't we agreed we would not do this?" he asked.

She looked back at him, with half a smile around the corners of her lips, like she was indulging a child. This infuriated him further.

"What's wrong with you? Why this sudden pro-life mania?" he demanded.

"I'm pro-choice," she replied, her voice calm and confident, "and this is my choice."

Her therapist said he had found her to be stable (as a conscientious mental-health professional, he never said "normal") for a long time now, and that he did not see why she should give up on being a mother.

"But we had *decided* parenthood was not for us. We discussed it before we got married. It was a rational, informed decision. This is not like her, Doctor. This is not *normal*. She's tricking you!" Santosh yelled.

"There's nothing abnormal about wanting to be a mother, Santosh," said the therapist in his most professional voice.

Santosh gave up trying to understand what was going on. He threw himself into his work. He spent all his time at the university, taking classes or just preparing for them in his office. He stopped inviting his students home. He would return very late and head straight to his study and work on his post-doctoral research. Bhagirati, on the other hand, grew cheerful and radiant, bearing her pregnancy with cinematic unreality. Hormones, sickness, food cravings, fatigue, moods – none of the usual idiosyncrasies of pregnancy touched her. She cooked and kept house with a gaiety that would surprise anyone who had known her earlier distaste for housewifery. But nothing surprised Santosh anymore, and he hardly noticed the sparkling clean house, the freshly cut flowers on his work desk or the delicacies she churned out, day after day.

One day, Bhagirati quietly knocked on the door of his study and said, "It's time." There was no shortness of breath, no panic or anxiety, and no hard-to-bear contractions that would cause her to scrunch up her glowing face. He drove her to the hospital and waited outside the delivery room. She had refused an epidural and was firm that it was to be a natural birth. They let him in half an hour later. The doctors and the nurses were amazed by the ease of it all. She lay on the bed smiling, with nothing but a few strands of hair pressed with dried sweat to show she had gone through labour. The baby, swathed in a soft white cloth, was in a crib next to her. Santosh looked at it and something inside him stirred. He looked away, wiping a tear.

*

She was dressed in flowy white silk. The fabric was embroidered with white thread, making its texture richer without interfering with its pristine whiteness. A strapless blouse – a slim tube-top – covered her shapely breasts, which were unbelievably firm without a bra. The lower part of the garment, worn as a dhoti, started just below the navel, exposing her delicate belly button, slender waist and flat abs. The loosely worn dhoti set off her toned thighs and calves. The white *odhani*, which was unattached to any other part of her clothing and barely hid any part of her body, hung loosely on her shoulders, swaying in the breeze. Her arms, bare except for the bracelets of jasmine at the wrists, were long and slender. Her shiny black hair cascaded luxuriantly down to her hips. Bhagirati was taller, slimmer, paler, softer of skin and more delicate of features than she had ever been. There was no sign of childbirth on her. She looked perfectly *Amar Chitra Katha*.

She sat on a large boulder, looking at the gently flowing river. He had followed her there after hearing the brief wail of the baby and a soft *plop*. He stood half covered by an outcrop of ferns and looked at her, resignation threatening to give in to grief on his face. She turned around and smiled at him.

"You know I'm fluid, I know no norm
I can turn icy or soothingly warm
I respond in kind to your ministrations
I bear your cares within my form."

He sat down and wept silently.

"Bathed in my waters my child will be pure
His place in the next world will be secure
Be it sedition or stealing a cow
Of all of his sins, he will be cured."

He did not look up.

THE BONESETTER

He was pontificating on the virtues of *desi* as opposed to allopathic medicine – a capitalist scam, a pharmaceutical conspiracy, an isolated and un-holistic ideology of healing, and so on and so forth – through clenched teeth, while she was trying to concentrate on the road. He had slipped on some broken eggs and had tried to break his fall with his left hand. There had been a snap as his hand twisted back under his weight. A swelling had developed in his forearm that looked like a large, two-yolked egg nestled under his skin. She stopped by the flexi-board to ask for directions, but as soon as she peeped out of the window, she realised she didn't need to. The bonesetter's was the grandest of *pakka* houses in the village. And it had a dusty white SUV parked in the front, just like she had been told.

He was a bonesetter. His father and grandfather had been bonesetters too. Like his father, he was also called Gandhi-*tata* – Grandfather Gandhi – and the few people in the village who had known his real name had forgotten it since he began setting bones. The thick tarp mat that marked the space of his bone-setting practice inside his one-room hut had also belonged to his grandfather. The mat had been white once, but he had always known it to be a watered-down coffee colour, with many blotches of darker hues all over. And, although he washed it clean with caustic soap every week, it always looked dull and grimy.

He sat on this mat, like his father and grandfather had done before him, crossing his legs so that the inverted "V" of one leg jutting straight out before his torso rested on the inverted "V" of the other, and the knees were almost stacked up. He massaged the sole of his left foot with his right hand – just as they had, too. This pose had earned his father the moniker of Gandhi-tata. Although his grandfather had had the same pose too and was in fact a contemporary of *the* Gandhi, no one had thought of calling him that because they hadn't actually known Gandhi's characteristic posture. It was only after newspapers brought the idiosyncrasies of personalities belonging to a region removed by hundreds of miles from their own, to spin images of the entire land mass as one nation, did anyone know enough to compare someone to a national figure. Thus, along with the mat, he had inherited the title and was known as Gandhi-tata, the bonesetter, despite being too young to be a grandfather.

Every morning, in the austerity of his humble hut, with incense sticks and handfuls of freshly plucked jasmine, he prayed to an array of portraits arranged in a line on the wall. The portraits of gods and goddesses of varying opulence and garishness of dress and jewellery had been inherited too, while the photographs of political leaders had been added by him. The fact that they belonged to his caste was of great pride to him. After his little ritual of worship, he sat down on the mat before his small wooden chest that also served as a table, and waited for patients. The chest contained a mortar and pestle, bowls with green pastes made from a secret herb he ground every evening for the next day's use, little bamboo sticks, strips of cloth and a tray of eggs.

While not exactly gregarious by nature, Gandhi-tata loved to narrate a story to his patients. It was the same story over and over again, but he never tired of telling it.

Once upon a time, there lived a king. He was greatly popular among his people, but was rather shy and limited his public interactions to the most cursory of *durbars*, which he conducted from a throne so high that people could not see him too clearly. He was never seen without his turban, which he wore low over his ears. In fact, no one ever saw him without his turban. Not even the queen, who, after a few failed attempts to get him to remove it, had left him in a huff, never to return. There was one exception though – the king's personal barber. And what did the barber see when he unwound this long strip of cloth from the king's head? Donkey ears! Long, tapering laminas – grey on the outside, pale pink on the inside, with a thin network of veins – that could never belong to a human. When did the king grow these ears? Was he born with them? Did they grow on him in his youth? No one knew. The barber, who came every week to give the king's head a massage, to trim his moustache and beard and cut his hair, was bound by oath on fear of death never to mention the ears to anyone. Having kept it to himself for many, many years, the barber, one day, felt he had to let it out somehow or he would die under the weight of this secret. So, he went deep into the forest, deeper than even the cowherds or hunters dared venture, and there he cupped his hands over the trunk of a large tree and began chanting *raja'n kiwi katti kiwi* – the king's ears are donkey's ears – *raja'n kiwi, katti kiwi*. After uttering this a hundred times, he felt purged of his painful secret and went back home feeling happier and lighter.

Those were the days when the kingdom was expanding, and the forest was constantly being cut down to meet the needs of civilisation. Soon, even the tallest tree in the deepest forest was felled to make way for a garden with fountains and statues. The wood of a certain tree was used to make a tabla set. But these tablas could only play one taal: the eight-beat *kaharva*! No matter what the fingers drummed on the tablas, it only rang out as dha – ge – na – te – na – ka – dhe – na – **the** – **ki** – **ing's** – **ears** – **are** – **don** – **key's** – **ears** – dha – ge – na – te – na – ka – dhe – na. That's how everyone found out.

The bonesetter would chuckle heartily as he concluded the story. Almost on cue, he would separate the egg whites to be mixed with the herb paste that would go on the broken arm or leg, before a thin bamboo stick would be placed on it for support and a strip of white cloth bound over it. His patients, too much in pain to be humoured by a funny story, most often did not react and simply bit down on their lips to brace themselves for the twisting and binding they were being subjected to. Those who felt obliged to react managed no more than a thin, mirthless *ha ha*.

In that largely agrarian community, where people worked the soil with their limbs, broken bones weren't rare. But the bonesetter's insistence on not charging for his services galled his wife. After the birth of a son, in spite of the thundering protests by men and women of the immediate and extended family, she had her tubes tied. "I'm the one who works like a mule on other people's land to feed us *mudde* and *saaru* twice a day. What does this wastrel of a husband make with all his bone-tying? Those louts don't even pay for the sticks that he binds their bones with. Sometimes, even the rupee coins he puts under the tapes are given by him. And what a waste of good eggs! For all the advice not to eat moringa while recovering, you'd think they would at least spare us their unwanted moringa. Freeloaders! He won't say a word to them. And who will feed more children? You?" she screamed at them. Either daunted by the volume of her screams or the logic of her words, they had left her alone.

The bonesetter owned a small, two-acre patch of land that, after several attempts to farm, had yielded nothing. While everyone's land grew *raagi*, corn, coconuts, sour and fibrous mangos for pickles, radishes, amaranth, fenugreek and moringa, his remained as barren as a menopausal bride. His land stood atop a knoll and the water never held. That wasn't all. One year, the little *raagi* that stood out like a sickly fox's tail was eaten by locusts; the next, the cobs came out lush green, but held no grain in them; then, once again, a fire that eluded everyone else's land appeared only on his. When this kept happening, they came to the only conclusion possible – his land was cursed. A *pooja*, where two large fatted rams were sacrificed to feed the entire village, didn't liberate it from the curse, and he simply gave up and went back to setting bones for free. His wife continued to slog away to feed the family of three.

Then came the news that, as part of the Asphalt Diamond project by the new government, the highway would pass through their village. And so it did. The land was quickly evaluated and bought by the government. As all the people of the village were of his caste, the political leader who represented them helped them cut through the red tape and ensured they all got their money on time. The villagers were only too eager to get rid of their land and buy houses in the shanty towns of the city. But, since Gandhi-tata's land began just where the asphalt lane ended, it wasn't bought. His land had meant nothing but dread and disappointment to him for a long time and Gandhi-tata barely noticed this new piece of bad news.

When the engineers arrived, they realised that his land stood at the exact elevation where the road would curve and run down on both sides, and was therefore best suited for parking their heavy equipment. Bulldozers, tarring machines, rolling machines, trucks and more trucks carrying stones, cement and whatnot came to park on his land. They paid him rent – in lakhs of rupees, every month. The work went on for years, and as his land stood bang in the middle of the 200-kilometre stretch, the company that had the contract to build the highway continued to park its equipment and vehicles there for a long, long time.

The bonesetter saw more money in a month than three generations of his family had in their combined lifetimes. In six months, he had bought an SUV: a white Scorpio that turned a dusty red every evening, owing to the road work. He washed it every morning with buckets of water pumped out from the newly installed borehole.

He built a three-room house where his hut had stood – three large, artless cubes of rooms – and painted all the walls gold. His bone-setting room at the back contained his pantheon, which was now gilded in brass, and his chest was replaced by a glass-topped table. In the room was a large revolving chair covered with *tharki* towels, on which he had to sit erect and not cross-legged. A cupboard held the sticks, the pastes and other paraphernalia. He even had an X-ray machine now. It was operated by his nephew, who had returned to the village from the city, where his parents had moved after selling their land to the road. The boy had failed his tenth standard exams and had got into trouble. He had gained a reputation as a peeping Tom and had been roughed up by jealous husbands and protective fathers of the women of his neighbourhood. His parents thought it best that he return to the village, where, under the watchful eyes of his now affluent uncle, he could learn a new trade. Gandhi-tata charged money for the X-ray. He held the film out to the patients and showed them where the bone was broken – information he and they had done without in the past.

The outer room had a large LED TV on which he watched the news – channels and channels of screaming yellow journalism in garish hues that went on all day and all night. His favourites were the prime-timers that recreated crime scenes. If patients arrived during the show, they would be led past him in the TV hall to the bone-setting room, where they would wait for him on moulded plastic chairs. When they passed him in the outer hall, he wouldn't so much as acknowledge their presence.

He still didn't charge them for setting their broken bones. But now, they bent down and touched his feet and offered him gifts of vegetables or wild honey or a chicken or liquor in tetrapacks. He wouldn't touch any of them. He wouldn't even look at them. They would leave their gifts on the floor, from where his wife picked them up and took them to the third room, where they slept. She continued to cook on an open fire outside by the back door. She wouldn't have one of those smoky, claustrophobic modern "kitchens". The old tarp mat had been folded and put away somewhere, and he didn't tell them the story of the king with donkey's ears anymore.

Then, his only son was run over by a bulldozer. His wife's tubes were promptly untied and, after three female foetuses were removed, the desired heir was born. This time, they had two, just to be safe. She had stopped working the land long ago.

Right next to the pantheon gallery, there was a picture of him posing with the most prominent political leader of his caste, who was now a big minister.

At the corner of the street, under the large banyan tree, there used to be the puncture shop. In the dirt outside the little wooden shed next to the truck tyres, a naked bulb had hung inside the tube of a car tyre slung on a Y-shaped stick to indicate the shop's business. The wooden board that read *Bharat puncher shop*, painted by hand in white letters that varied in size, was barely noticed in the day and did not show in the night. What showed was the crescent of light reflecting on the inner curve of the tube and the bright bulb shining like a star when seen from a distance. Similar to most small businesses in the village, the puncture-*anna*'s prosperity had shot up considerably ever since the road work had begun. But eyebrows had been raised for him alone, and, upon Gandhi-tata's gentle request, he had left town overnight with bag and baggage.

The space thus vacated was now occupied by a large hoarding. The flexi-sheet had, at its centre, the legend *Gandhi-tata bon setar* printed on it in a cursive font. Below that, in smaller letters, was written *100%*, and the sheet had the images of a toothless, smiling Gandhi, the stern, staring face of the bonesetter himself, two lions charging at each other and a large red rose in each of its four corners.

He took no notice of Sylvia as he twisted and turned her husband's hand to ascertain the spot of the fracture. His wife peeped in from the inside room and stared suspiciously at the open-haired woman in pants. When the bonesetter was done tying up her husband's arm, he said, "Don't eat drumsticks for a month, sir." He looked at Sylvia for a moment, but turned back to her husband and began with a smile, "Do you know the story of the king with the donkey's ears? Once upon a time…"

VENISON

After a gap of fifteen minutes, the clanging and the banging began afresh. Shaila tried peeping over the wall that divided the backyard of her house from Rukmini's. She couldn't see anything, though the noises kept coming. It had been a while since Rukku was last possessed, and this time, the fury of the spirit that inhabited her body seemed to be making up for lost time. The gibberish of her screams contained a sprinkling of intelligible phrases, mostly Dakhni expletives. *"Aan-de…sob haram khoran-ku maar'k sata-toon…"* she raged in a guttural voice that wasn't her own. Shaila imagined she must be frothing at the mouth as she shook with an epilepsy-like seizure, like the time she had seen her in one of her phases. She must be taking breaks from the quivering to fling pots and pans at the wall and curse her mother.

When, months ago, Shaila and her husband Sujeeth had moved into the village, fresh from the city, and discovered that their landlord's daughter had a history of demonic possession, they had tried to help by insisting her parents seek psychiatric intervention. But the sixteen-year-old Rukku's elders had dismissed it gruffly, even though they forgave the city slickers for their outrageous suggestion.

"Take her to a mad-hospital, she says!" the mother muttered to the bedridden grandmother. "To have my daughter put in chains and given electric shocks on her head, so she just sits and drools all her life! Who will marry her then?"

"Leave them be. They mean well," said the peaceable old lady. "That is how city folks are. The boy is from Kerala or somewhere, isn't he? And she is a *Hiremath* too. Who would have allowed such a marriage here? Wonder what her parents had to say about it. School-read children these days don't even seek their parents' permission for marriage. But nice boy, he is… very polite."

"I cannot even pronounce his full name," said Rukku's mother, without realising that the sly old lady had changed the topic to an easier, gossipier one which she knew her daughter-in-law wouldn't resist. "At least Sujeeth is a Hindu name. Although, I assume Hindus in Kerala are nothing like us."

"We must invite them to lunch sometime. After all, no one ever visits us anymore. To think we are Brahmin, but we live like outcastes." The older lady's voice cracked as she spoke the last sentence.

The Kulkarnis were indeed shunned by the rest of the village community. No one visited them and they weren't invited to the social functions of any other Brahmin household in the village. And that was how Shaila Hiremath and Sujeeth Jacob Kaniyamparambil had ended up being their tenants. The couple had met and married in Bangalore. After spending the first few years of their marriage there, like any other IT couple, they had decided they'd had enough of the traffic and the pollution and the never-ending threats by the municipal corporation to chop down more trees – which would die down after the citizens protested, only to come up again for a different development plan – and they'd had enough of what they deemed the unexamined life. Sujeeth sought solace in tending to their terrace garden and he reminisced fondly of childhood visits to his uncle's rubber plantation in Wayanad. While the slopes of the hills grew rubber, the valleys had paddy, and he had felt great joy in working alongside the farmhands in ankle-deep mud there. Slowly, the dream of becoming a farmer himself took root in his head. And Shaila wanted what he wanted. Together, they pored over the many back-to-the village success stories on the Internet and watched videos on YouTube of how engineers-turned-farmers had improvised simple technology to mechanise their farming processes. They sold their car and whatever furniture they had and brought their possessions down to a few suitcases of clothes and books.

After some feeling around, they arrived in Kanas, which was close to where her family came from. Life is simpler when urban people go to live in villages in linguistic regions other than their own. The moral difference they display is quickly ascribed to the otherness of the region they come from. Most of their aberrations are forgiven or overlooked, and being patronised as an exotic species is the worst that can happen to them. But when they speak the language of that place, they are no longer the other. Seen to belong, they are inadvertently subject to judgement; they are slotted by caste and their urban corruptions are more keenly scrutinised. For Shaila, that was a real fear. She had grown up in Delhi, but Kanas was in the region to which she traced her heritage. Shaila was very close to her father. While he had always been supportive of her choices, he was apprehensive about his very urban daughter moving to the village. "It's not as idyllic as you imagine it, *tangi*. You'll feel out of place there," he tried warning her. But he knew she was very stubborn in matters concerning Sujeeth and eventually he stopped trying to deter her. Instead, he assured her that he'd be there for them if they ever needed anything. He had spoken to a relative who had arranged for them to get a four-acre plot of farmland in Kanas on lease for a good price.

The land did not have a house, and while they constructed a basic structure for themselves on it, they had to find accommodation in the village. Shaila dreaded being in the densely populated Lingayat neighbourhood. Although they chose to drop the "Jacob" from Sujeeth's name when introducing themselves to people, she was worried it would be impossible to hide their interreligious marriage from "her" people for too long. So, when they found out that there was a house available with the Kulkarnis, who lived a little away from the cluster of Brahmin houses, flanked by the Muslim colony, they had chosen to take it instantly.

Rukku's condition was not the only reason the Kulkarnis were ostracised by the villagers. Being possessed did not raise many eyebrows in a place where ghost stories hung in the air like the omnipresent red dust blown up from the fields by the hot winds. Most of the houses in the village were very old and had sheltered many generations of families who had lived and died there. The Lingayat burial ground that had earlier been on the outskirts of the village had been pulled into its map recently. The land it stood on was reclaimed by the prominent Banajiga family that owned it, to build a pre-university college in memory of its recently departed dowager, Gurawwa Gursiddappa Balikai. But the dead drove a hard bargain and it was agreed that the graves would be allowed to remain and only a cluster of tamarind trees on the land would be cut down to make way for the college building.

People continued to die, and corpses continued to be buried in what was now called the "college graveyard". Soon, the college simply came to be known as the "graveyard college".

Teachers took tea breaks whenever the noise of the drumming and firecrackers accompanying a funeral cortège cut into their lectures, waiting for the burial to be over before resuming their class. As the upright, cross-legged corpses, bedecked in flowers, rode their biers into the college graveyard, the stiffness in their joints somehow eluded their necks and they nodded in wholehearted agreement to being brought to their final resting place by the pall-bearers walking on uneven ground. The students gradually got over their fear of the dead. Some even mocked the bobbing heads of the corpses, eliciting guarded teenage laughter. They willed themselves to do what the lack of will made the dead people do, and thus experienced the metaphysics of life by a nod of the head. The difference between a dead and a live rabbit is only a hare's breath, after all.

They would later scrounge for coins flung by the mourners around fresh mounds of earth, to buy themselves cigarettes and sweets. Thus, the science and commerce college was inadvertently teaching philosophy to the youngsters of the village. While that was the story of the Lingayat death ritual, the diversity of departed souls was maintained by the Muslim burial ground at a distance and the Brahmin crematorium down by the stream.

*

When one day Rukku flung her head back and stared with ghostly white eyes, her body jerking grotesquely, her family knew exactly what to do. They took her to the *acharya*, who lit bonfires and flung rice and vermilion, amongst other things, into the flames, muttered mantras and sprinkled holy water on her and got the spirit to scoot. That wasn't what caused them to be ostracised, of course. In fact, everyone in the village looked upon them with sympathy, albeit indifferent. It was the sort of thing that could happen to anybody. But the spirit returned after a month, and since Rukku was a student of the graveyard college, the family wondered if it was a Lingayat ghost that had possessed her and the Brahmin priest's mantras hadn't been strong enough for the garlic-fed spirit. They took her to a Lingayat elder, trained in the occult crafts, who spoke sternly to the spirit, insisting repeatedly that it take to its heels, until Rukku passed out. He gave her a sachet of holy ash and an amulet and sent her away with the assurance that she would be well henceforth.

But she was possessed again at the next new moon and, when she began mouthing expletives in Dakhni, they realised that their worst fears had come true. They secretly took her to Hussainsaab at the Jod-Gummat durgah – the mausoleum with the twin domes – who placed a heavy block of stone on her head and ordered her to hold it up. Rukku stood there with her eyes flashing crimson rage while he blew frankincense smoke on her and whipped her with a peacock-feather fan. An hour into the treatment, Rukku dropped the rock and went limp. Hussainsaab sat back in a trance and spoke into the ether. "*Kon tume? Kon karya? Kyawn? Ran-deo jao tume…jao…jate-ki-nai? Jate ki NAI? Kya hona tumna?*"

The other side of the conversation wasn't heard, but Hussainsaab fell back suddenly, as if flung by a great force, and slowly came back to his senses. He gave his verdict: "Yes. She is indeed possessed by the spirit of one of our people. He is the worst I have seen. Won't leave easily. He was tied to a tree and left to die of hunger by his enemies. He is asking to be fed. Give her mutton when she is possessed next. He will leave on his own when he has had his fill." With more powders and amulets and warnings of how not to incur the wrath of the spirit, he sent them away. They were determined to keep it a secret, but Pinjaar Pakirappa, to whom they had gone seeking the unmentionable food for the hungry tenant of their daughter's body, had a tattler of a wife. Soon word of the Kulkarnis' daughter's mutton consumption had ears ringing and tongues wagging in Kanas.

Heresy and hearsay are closely connected. So, while the pollution of interreligious demonic possession could have been forgiven, the real-world breach of a food taboo had caused the family to be ostracised from the village. After many dirty looks from neighbours and having been refused admission into the holy *matha* on *aradhani* day, Rukku's father decided to move his family of five – his son, daughter, wife and aged mother – from the joint family home that they shared with his cousins in the clustered Brahmin colony to their new house a distance away from the rest of the village. When a plot of land had become available cheaply a few years ago, he had had the foresight to buy it and build on it. He planned to rent it out as a source of income as he was up for retirement from his job as clerk in the Grameena bank. It was a set of two tiny one-bedroom-hall-and-kitchen units, arranged like matchboxes stacked together, with a backyard divided between the houses by a low wall. Their tenants had vacated recently, and they occupied the larger of the two houses.

Pinjaar Pakirappa continued to deliver spicy mutton curry to the Kulkarnis whenever asked. He took great pleasure in adding variety to his deliveries. "Have made red *girvi* today. Will bring green *girvi* the next time." The Kulkarnis couldn't care less about the colour of the gravy as long as the spirit that held their daughter was satisfied with it and left them in peace for the next fortnight.

No one wanted to live in their other house anymore. So, when Shaila and Sujeeth asked to rent it, the Kulkarnis were pleasantly surprised and didn't bother them with too many personal questions. When Shaila volunteered that they sometimes cooked non-vegetarian food, they didn't seem to care about the additional pollution to the already polluted house. But, one afternoon, Rukku's mother, out of irrepressible curiosity, called out to Shaila over the backyard wall.

"I know Sujeeth is from Kerala. But you are Hiremath, no? How come you are non-vegetarian?"

"No, aunty-*ri*, I was raised a vegetarian. But I started eating poultry and seafood in college. My parents didn't mind. And Sujeeth has always been non-vegetarian."

"What caste is he?"

"In Kerala, everyone eats meat." Shaila evaded the question.

The woman was satisfied with the idea that Shaila was being a good wife by attending to her husband's gastronomic needs, but she was still curious about Shaila's own habits. "So, you eat mutton and all?" she persisted.

"No, aunty-*ri*. I don't eat red meat."

"What is red meat?"

"Meat of mammals. Animals that give birth to young ones and breastfeed their offspring. Goats, sheep, buffaloes, co—"

Aunty sucked in her breath violently and began sobbing. "It's such a sin...such a sin! To what do we owe this karma that our Rukku has to commit this sin...of eating the flesh of mothers and babies...?"

"Aunty-*ri*...it's all right. It's only natural. Please calm yourself." Shaila didn't know what else to say to pacify her.

"But…it is not Rukku. It's that monster that possesses her that the sin belongs to." Aunty wiped her tears, placating herself.

Later, when Shaila recounted the conversation to Sujeeth, he said it was a sensitive topic for the Kulkarnis and they mustn't discuss food habits with them, and Shaila agreed – as she did with everything he said. Since then, Shaila had maintained a polite distance from the Kulkarnis' gastro-spiritual matters, offering sympathy only when asked for.

*

Today, when Rukku began her tantrum anew, Shaila knew someone would call Pinjaar Pakirappa on his cell phone, and he'd rush over with the day's special, and things would be back to normal by the afternoon. She had not slept well the previous night, gripped by an unexplainable fear regarding Sujeeth, and felt too drained to bear the noise from next door. Sujeeth had left for the farm on his bicycle after breakfast. Normally, Shaila stayed back to finish the housework and cook and pack lunch for the two of them. She would then ride her scooter to join Sujeeth at the farm. They would eat together and she would tinker around a bit before sitting down under a tree to read a book. He and Mudkappa, the farmhand, would busy themselves all day, weeding and watering the seedlings. She would leave for home on her scooter after a while and he would return at dusk on his bicycle.

Today, she didn't feel up to cooking and decided to take a walk instead. She had walked a distance on the dirt track towards the college graveyard when she saw Sujeeth cycling towards her from the other side, raising red dust. She waited for him to join her. "What happened?" she asked when he drew near and jumped off his bicycle.

"Mudkappa…bad hangover…too much moonshine last night…could barely stand," Sujeeth panted.

Shaila waited for him to recover his breath before asking him further questions.

"So, what did you do?"

"I fed him water and electrolytes from my emergency kit and put him on a tractor back home. There wasn't much work to be done, so I called it a day too. What about you?"

"It is one of Rukku's days. Couldn't take it. Decided to walk."

He nodded sympathetically. They began walking together in silence while he pushed his bicycle along. As if by a prior decision, they stopped in front of the run-down tin-roofed shed with the missing windows. The padlocked door protected an empty shell of a room. While the walls looked grey with dead mould, the legend *Clara Memorial Convent School*, painted in neatly stencilled brushstrokes on its side wall, remained un-erased. They sat on the platform in silence for a while.

"Sujeeth…"

"Hmmm…?"

"You remember that phone call you got at five in the morning last June…you cut it immediately and walked out with your phone and shut the door behind you…"

"Do you have to start that all over again?"

"No, but you haven't told me—"

"Shut up!"

She sat gazing into space. After a minute, he put his arm around her shoulder.

"Who is Clara? What is her story?" he said in a placating voice.

"Christianly routine and covered in glory?" she continued the rhyme.

"What does she happen to be doing in Kanas?"

"Giving her bit for education cess."

"Or simply inhabiting a hoary allegory?" He laughed, concluding the limerick Sylvia had composed when she had visited them a while ago. She had been surprised to see the shed and thought it odd for a place like that to exist in Kanas, a village that couldn't possibly inspire any proselytising or edifying interest in the most determined of missions. Shaila laughed with him.

"Let's go home," he said. They began walking.

"I haven't cooked anything," she said.

"It's all right. I'll cook today. What do we have?"

"Nothing."

"It's Monday. The *santi* must have started. Let's go get vegetables and supplies."

They picked up a large cloth bag and rode the scooter to the village square, which turned into an open market every Monday, with vendors spreading their wares on mats on the ground. Sujeeth got busy haggling over the price of cucumbers in his Malayalam-mixed Bangalore-Kannada, and the vegetable vendor covered her mouth with the loose end of her sari and giggled. Shaila rolled her eyes and walked over to where she knew Hasheena would be with her *ghamat* sprouts.

Ghamat is an unpleasant food odour; it can be anything from rancid to damp to sour; it is a subtly repulsive smell, unlike the sharper non-food stenches. Hasheena transported her sprouts to the market in a plastic sheath. With not much room to breathe, they accumulated ghamatness. Hasheena, in selling sprouted pulses, displayed the inevitable enterprise of poor village women. Shaila didn't know much about her, but it was easy to guess that she and her family owned no land – certainly not fertile, water-fed land that could grow vegetables. Perhaps she did manual labour on the other six days; her stick-thin figure and the mud in the cracks of her palms suggested it. She certainly did not want to forgo the chance of participating in the weekly market where the village people saw more cash change hands than they would hold in their own lives. She usually got three kinds of pulses – green gram, moth bean and horse gram. Soaked overnight and allowed to germinate the next day, they swelled up to almost three times their original size. Bought by weight and sold by volume, the shift in measure was what contained her living. The odour of the sprouts could be overcome by adding an extra pinch of garam masala and cooking an extra five minutes with the lid off.

"Awo bhabhi, kya hona?" Hasheena called out to Shaila cheerily. The first time Shaila had gone to shop from her, Hasheena had eyed her with suspicion. What kind of grown woman wears trousers? But word had perhaps spread since then and she had realised that Shaila was a respectable married woman, just like her. Shaila, for her part, had got over the strangeness of being addressed as sister-in-law and, in fact, had come to like it. Today, she bought a measure each of the three kinds of sprouts for thirty rupees, deciding the lunch menu.

Rukku's spiritual tenant, who had had his prescribed meal, had left her and all was quiet in the house. Shaila and Sujeeth took a long nap after lunch. When she woke up, Shaila was still dazed from unhappy dreams. She drank a cup of black filter coffee – something that was hard to source in the village and was hence ordered online, to be delivered to the address of her cousin in the closest big town – and decided to take a walk again. Alone.

She walked by the side of the dirt track that led from their house to the highway. She walked on the side of the tarmac. The undulating landscape opened out for miles on end on either side of her. It was a clear, cloudless day and the pink, sinking sun hung dangerously close to the earth on her right. She could see windmills in the distance on her left and the palashas, having shed their leaves, were bare branches sprouting orange blooms. There were small blue spots here and there – water bodies that wouldn't last beyond the coming summer. Unlike Bangalore's streets, where one had to jostle with people to walk, here, she was the only one on the road for miles. She walked under the tunnel-like canopy that the tamarind and banyan trees on either side of the road had formed. The open fields were blocked from view now and the forest seemed to engulf her. The trees on the side of the road had horizontal white and rust-red stripes on their trunks, marking them as belonging to the forest department – not to be felled without permission. "Such Lingayat country," she said to herself. "Even the trees wear *vibhuti* here." She smiled to herself as the mists in her head began to clear slowly. It was beginning to get dark now and, against her better judgement, she walked on.

*

They had come to the village when the country was in the throes of an economic bloodletting cure for fiscal anaemia. There had been mayhem and panic in the bigger towns and cities, but Kanas had been relatively insulated from it as most transactions here happened on credit. Since their needs were few and everything was so much cheaper, they managed all right with the little cash they had on them. If the corn and the coconuts come well and we are able to break even this year, we may be able to invest in a hothouse next year and grow bell peppers, courgettes and broccoli, and sell them to organic restaurants in Goa, Shaila thought to herself. Our savings must last us a couple of years in the meanwhile. We could even have a few cows. I hope that will keep Sujeeth busy and help him get over whatever it is that he was doing behind my back in Bangalore. Perhaps I should call Sylvia, one of these days. She is his oldest friend and might know something I don't. Good that we hit it off when we met at our wedding. It's been a while since I spoke to her. The last I heard from her, she was talking of marrying a free-range chicken farmer and moving in with him somewhere in the hinterlands. Was saying something about passive income and peace for writing…

It was only by the light of a passing bus that she realised how dark it was and that she must head back. She remembered she didn't have her phone – not that it was of much use there, as there was no signal, but it was a good feeling to know it was handy – and her fears returned all of a sudden. Although she often craved and needed solitude, she knew the importance of *ulu* – human thoroughfare. Solitude is beautiful in a safe, enclosed space. But out in an open, lonesome place, she wanted to see other people. Fear of individuals or men in groups gathered at the back of her mind. Her belief that humans were innately violent and greedy, and the only thing that kept them from wanton acts of cruelty was the fear of the judgement of others, came back to her, sharp and jagged. The project of culture was to internalise this judging eye and keep people from hurting each other even when they could get away with it. But culture was a luxury for most and arguing oneself out of the instinct to rob, kill and rape could be a waste of time for many. Hence, people found safety in numbers – even if the numbers were made up of strangers.

She only had the lights of passing vehicles to guide her back. All the horror stories of crimes in different parts of the world that she had scrolled through on Facebook and commented self-righteously upon in the past few days flashed before her eyes. She did not feel the tears roll down her cheeks as she walked fast. She heard footsteps behind her. She turned to see the beam of a flashlight following her. She hastened her steps and the footsteps became faster too. She broke into a run knowing well that whoever was behind her might easily outrun her.

"Madam!" yelled the voice behind her, and cackled.

She ran even faster.

"O madam, wait…madam!"

"Madam!"

"Madam! Madam! Bhabhi! Madam! Bhabhi…Bhabhi… Shaila…Shailu…Shailu…"

The voice sounded like it was coming from the other side of a large volume of water. She opened her eyes, feeling woozy and parched, to find herself in the tiny bedroom of their Kanas home. Sujeeth was sitting next to her looking deeply concerned.

"What happ—?"

He held a glass of water to her lips before she could speak any further. She drank it and sat up on the bed, leaning back.

"Anil called me on the phone a while ago to say you had fainted on the road. I drove over and picked you up and brought you home. What's wrong with you?"

"Who is Anil?" she asked, puzzled.

"He belongs to the Samaari tribe and lives in the settlement behind our land. I run into him every day on the farm. He saw you walking in the dark and tried to talk to you, but he says you began running and, before he could catch up with you, you had fainted. He was worried people would think he had done something to you, so he called me immediately. Thank goodness. What were you thinking, Shaila? Why didn't you tell me where you were going? And why didn't you take your phone?"

"I'm sorry. Guess I wasn't thinking. I'm really sorry."

He held her close as she cried silently.

"I won't do it again," she sniffed.

"It's all right…I was worried about you."

After she recovered, she asked for another glass of water.

"What did Anil want with me? Why was he calling out to me?"

"He wanted to ask you if you would be interested in buying some venison from him."

"Venison?"

"Yes. They set some traps and caught a large deer. It was too big for his family, and he wanted to sell some of the meat."

"What did you say to him?"

"I refused. We shouldn't buy hunted meat. They hunt and trap for themselves now, which is fine. If people begin buying it, they will begin to hunt more recklessly."

While it was illegal to hunt openly, the forest guards let the Samaari and Manchi tribes trap small mammals and birds, usually in exchange for a small portion of the meat. If the Manchi, who ate pigs, cats and rats, and lived in dirty hovels in the unwanted spaces outside the village, caught deer, the guards accepted raw meat from them and took it home to their wives, who would cook it with mutton recipes. If it was the Samaari, the upwardly mobile erstwhile nomadic tribe that traced its roots back to North Indian warriors, who made the kill, the guards did not mind a share in the cooked meat, and sometimes participated in the revelry in their colonies, where home-brewed moonshine flowed freely. Most of the forest around the farmlands in the village had been converted to eucalyptus or acacia plantations – softwood trees commissioned by paper factories. The deer could not eat their leaves. And the trees originally meant for draining swamps had made sure that the dry plains they grew on could not hold on to one pond or puddle in their vicinity. The hungry and thirsty deer naturally pranced over to the green fields and were trapped by farmers. Sujeeth and Shaila had been worried by frequent deer raids too. They had fenced their land with old saris that could be bought for twenty rupees each – haggled down to fourteen if one was determined. But the deer were good jumpers.

After her ordeal, Shaila ran a fever for a few days. She felt weak and could barely walk. Sujeeth looked after her in that time. He cooked and cleaned before leaving for the farm. He put a flask of hot ginger tea by her bed and asked her to call him if she needed anything. He took the scooter rather than the bicycle so he could hurry back if she wanted him for something. He came home for lunch in the middle of the day to check on her. It was nearly a week before she regained her strength and got back to her routine. She hugged Sujeeth before he left for work that morning. He had been so gentle and caring when she was ill. Perhaps she could write off his little moral lapse as a one-off error. He was very ethical, after all. His decision not to buy hunted meat was absolutely right. And, anyway, things were about to improve for them. They were far away from the maddening city and were living by the sweat of their brow like they had always dreamed. There was fresh air and good vibes all around. A sharp rap on the door disrupted her thoughts.

"Shaila!" Sujeeth's voice sounded urgent.

She opened the door. "What happened? Are you all right? It's barely been an hour since you left."

"Quick. Shut the door." He drew out a heavy, bloodied cloth sack from inside a plastic bag.

"Wha—?"

"Shhh! It's venison," he whispered hoarsely.

"But I thought you said we mustn't buy—"

"I didn't buy it. I caught it. The deer had been raiding the farm continuously all of last week. Nearly an acre of corn is gone. After agonising over it for days, Mudkappa and I decided to set a trap. We didn't mean to kill it. We thought we'd set it free in the morning. We hoped to scare it into not returning. But the dogs had got to it before we found it."

"Oh no…it's horrible. It's horrible."

"I know, Shailu. But it's dead now and, rather than throw it away and waste its death, I thought it better to eat it. I shared it with Mudkappa and Anil and some Manchi men."

"Who skinned it and cut it up?"

"I did."

"How did you know how to do it?"

"I watched a video on the Internet."

Shaila went into their bedroom and shut the door behind her. Sujeeth knew not to disturb her when she wanted to be left alone to think. She came out after some time with reddened eyes but a calm demeanour.

"*Kond paapa, tind parihaara,*" she said in a soft but firm voice. Atone for the sin of killing by eating your kill.

She did a quick search on the Internet and, accompanied by ginger, garlic, cumin, green chilli, coriander, star anise, cinnamon, cardamom, black pepper, onion, coconut milk, mint and limes, she prepared to atone. The aroma of the curry wafted through the house, overpowering their senses with a mad, craving, gripping desire to purge, to confess, to love. He gathered her in his arms and looked into her eyes with tears in his.

"I'm sorry for Bangalore," he said.

She wept as she hugged him back. "And I'm sorry for asking."

That evening, as they were about to begin eating, Sujeeth said, "Do you think we should give some to Rukku?"

"But she is not possessed today. The meat is for the spirit. She wouldn't eat it herself."

"You could ask."

Shaila hesitated. "Rukku's mother is away seeking treatment for the oedema in her feet. I have never spoken to Rukku directly. She has a wild look in her eyes…it is a little scary…"

"Then ask her father."

Shaila went over to the Kulkarnis' and gingerly knocked on the partially open door.

"Uncle?" she called out softly. There was no answer. She knocked again. "Uncle-*ri*…"

A steel tumbler was flung at the door from inside and landed near Shaila's feet with a resounding clang.

"*Maar'k sata-toon!*" Rukku screamed from within in a male voice.

BLUE BARREL

Reshma wants to wash her hair today. It's been over ten days since she washed it last. She doesn't have to prepare herself for her school friend's visit anymore. He has stopped coming. They don't talk on the phone either. They didn't do that even when he visited her regularly. Theirs was never that kind of a relationship. There were no long, sigh-filled phone conversations, no late-night texting, no looking deep into each other's eyes, no eating out and no exchanging of gifts. She simply stole water and bathed herself before he came, and they quietly made love in the darkness of the tin shed that was her home. Daddy, who would be lounging around the room in his *lungi*, would smile at the boy when he arrived and ask after his parents' health before grabbing his crutches and limping out to leave the young couple alone. He would sit outside on a broken stool and smoke a *beedi*, pretending not to be standing guard.

Reshma would push the blue barrel against the PVC door to cover the large crack in it once Daddy stepped out. Mummy would be away cooking and cleaning in the several big houses in the next street – most possibly in her school friend's home. That's probably how he knew when to visit her. How long had it been since his last visit? Three years? Four? Who kept count? He was married now. Reshma washed her hair for herself these days. She has thick, straight, back-length hair. Mummy hasn't been forcefully rubbing oil in it and tying it in tight braids since she was admitted to that big school. That was a long time ago. She has been leaving it down since then, only tying it into a high ponytail when it's hotter than usual. She isn't too bothered to brush or oil it either. She trims it herself when it gets too long. The carelessly tossed hair is becoming of the rest of her personality.

Her home in the shanty town, near the big traffic signal, is strategically located for stealing water from the water tanks that ply that road to fill the oversized sumps in the bungalows of the gated communities a kilometre ahead. It is one of those signals where most vehicles have to stop thrice – twice if it is a light traffic day – before they can cross. The tankers that had to take a left at the signal always made for the flank to facilitate a smooth turn without having to make horns blare. That usually gave Reshma enough time to drag the huge blue plastic barrel from her door to the road, place it under the tank's jutting pipe and turn the valve. The drivers of these tankers, who would most often be looking at the traffic light impatiently, were too distracted to notice a girl stealing a few litres of water from the back of the tanker. Even so, her father hopped down to the street to block the tanker's rear-view mirror. Reshma was always careful to close the valve before the truck drove off.

The family got its water from the common municipal tap, just like everyone else in their colony. Mummy stood in the queue at the crack of dawn to collect a few buckets and plastic pots of water. Reshma also helped her when she could. But that water was for drinking and cooking, and too dear to be spilt on luxuries like washing hair. They managed to save a bit at the end for a quick, frugal body-only bath every once in two days or so. Daddy forewent even that to allow Reshma a few extra mugfuls now and then. Then Reshma had been asked to wash her hair with medicated shampoo when she had joined that school and had been infested by lice. That's when she had devised a plan to steal the tanker water. As a child, she stole water in a small plastic bucket. Later, long after the lice were gone, her school friend's special interest in her had made her continue the practice and she had got the blue barrel.

Reshma must have been around five when Daddy's autorickshaw came under a cement mixer that crushed his leg. He barely made it alive. When the auto drivers' association made a big scene outside their office and threatened to go on a citywide strike, the construction company that owned the mixer paid to have his jagged stub of a shin trimmed to an even shape and stitched up. It also paid for his crutches. Daddy lay in bed for several months, attended to by Mummy. He went back to drink when his medicines stopped and began beating Mummy again. The blows weren't as hard as before, as balancing on one foot, with one arm holding a crutch, didn't give a man much leverage at wife-beating. It was mostly psychological. Suddenly, Mummy seemed to realise the farce of it and changed from being a quietly suffering wife to one who had had enough. One day, she struck back and sent him reeling to the floor. He lost his two front teeth from the impact, and the will to hit her.

After that, he began spending his time sitting around the house and smoking *beedies*, when he had them. He spoke to Reshma sometimes, but was mostly quiet. For her, he had the kindest voice. Mummy, who had once slunk around the house quivering in fear of her auto-driver husband, now stepped out and got a job cleaning houses. She wasn't hostile to him though. Nor did she rub her new-found independence in his face. She didn't chuck him out in a bid for vengeance. Even if he was a cripple, she thought it a good idea to have a man about the house, especially when there was a little daughter to be raised in a neighbourhood like theirs. She made sure he got a couple of meals a day and a tetrapack or two of cheap whisky, and let him be. When Reshma grew older, she began attending to his meals and Mummy didn't have to concern herself with him anymore. The role of husband rendered null and father vestigial, Daddy was neither indignant nor grateful at being allowed to outlive his use, and remained opinionless and out of everyone's way.

Mummy took Reshma with her sometimes when she went to clean the houses in Good Earth Community. Those were nice houses – neat, two-storey structures built of rammed-earth bricks made of local mud and upcycled wood. They had sloping tiled roofs, solid banisters, terracotta floors and winding stairs to mezzanine libraries. Many of them had open courtyards with potted succulents and bonsai palms and Buddha statuettes; they had rainwater harvesting apparatuses and solar water heaters on the terrace; they had brass bells and hanging oil lamps; they had framed drawings and paintings made by one or the other member of the family. Reshma felt small and shy in them.

The house owners were kind and offered the little girl jaggery sweets and cane toys. Veena aunty, in particular, was very sweet to her. Her son was the same age as Reshma and she encouraged them to play together. It was her husband, Jacob uncle, who suggested that Mummy send her to school with their Juju. At first, Mummy thought they were joking. It was a time long before educational policy compelled hoity-toity schools to scramble for loopholes to sneak through before grudgingly relenting to taking in a percentage of the neighbourhood riff-raff, and Mummy couldn't believe that her daughter could aspire to attend such a school.

But Jacob uncle was serious. "Well, *molé*, would you like to go to school with your best friend?" he asked Reshma, and she stared at the floor and played with the loose end of Mummy's sari. They took care of the admission formalities and paid her fees. "Veena Natarajan" was put in the space for "Parent/ Guardian" in the form. Juju had his father's surname, however. Veena aunty spoke to a neighbour and arranged for her daughter Sylvia's old clothes to be handed down to Reshma, so she would not stick out among her classmates. But stick out she did, as she did not speak English. Although with Veena aunty and Jacob uncle's help she learned it eventually, she never gained the unconscious ease of ownership with which the language rolled off the tongues of her classmates. It also didn't help that Sylvia was in the same class as her. She did not do anything to make Reshma feel uncomfortable. She was too busy wool-gathering when she wasn't reading a book to care about needling Reshma about her hand-me-downs. It was just that all the others had already seen Sylvia in the clothes that Reshma now wore, and when they hid their knowing expressions, Reshma cringed internally.

Her only solace was being with Juju. He seemed as bored with the classes as she was and didn't seem to care for what the teacher said. He couldn't read too well and failed all spelling "dictation" quizzes. They both ended up together on the last bench, where they sat and daydreamed or drew with their crayons while the teachers held class on battles and daffodils and squares on hypotenuses. Sometimes Sylvia joined them on the back bench during the science period, hid a storybook in the pages of her textbook and read quietly while pretending to listen to the teacher.

Over the years, Sylvia's clandestine reading went from the Hardy Boys to Agatha Christie to Márquez and Rushdie, while Reshma's constant failing of exams was attributed to her lack of application, and Juju was diagnosed with dyslexia. Veena aunty and Jacob uncle took Juju out of school and hired a specially qualified tutor to homeschool him. Juju also took arts-based therapy twice a week and spent two months every year on Jacob's family lands in Wayanad.

They offered to continue to pay for Reshma's schooling, although now they didn't take much interest in her homework and grades. They were as sweet and kind as ever, but Mummy felt burdened by a strange sense of guilt: could her daughter's poor performance at school be seen as ingratitude towards their benefactors? Reshma continued to attend school for a few more months after Juju left, but she felt tortuously lonely without him, and the lessons that had seemed like someone else's problem all along began to feel like personal reprimands. She eventually dropped out in the middle of her seventh standard. Veena aunty and Jacob uncle didn't bother convincing her to stay. She stopped going to Good Earth Community with Mummy, but continued to receive Sylvia's old clothes, which went from pretty sequinned dresses and brightly coloured tops with Powerpuff Girls and Barbie motifs to oversized pullovers and T-shirts in solid greys and dull blues, loose denims, Khaadi kurtas and cotton trousers. She even had wrap-around skirts, checked shorts and some kind of nightwear, but Mummy declined to take them for Reshma. She wore what she was sent without comment. The clothes set off her slender-boned, tall figure, which, combined with her loosely worn hair, gave her an intellectual look.

Reshma stayed home and cooked for herself and Daddy. She watched TV sometimes. She tried but could not mix with the girls in her colony. She didn't know what to say to them and they didn't like her for the inadvertent sartorial difference she displayed and the fact that she had briefly received the benevolence of the more fortunate.

When she was about sixteen, Mummy got her a job in a garment factory. It was around that time that Juju suddenly turned up at her house. They hadn't seen each other in years, and he looked quite different now. He was tall and broad-shouldered and there was a hint of a moustache above his lips. He wore glasses too. But something about his expression caught her eye. She invited him into the tin shed where Daddy was playing a video game on his phone. "Oh, Reshma's school friend, no? Come in, come in, sir. How are your parents? They have been most kind to our family," he said as way of greeting. "Please sit, sir. Sit and talk," he said, and got up and limped away.

Reshma didn't know what to say. Their friendship had always been about sitting together quietly and sharing a wordless despair about academics. They had understood each other very well, but had never bothered to articulate it.

"What?" Reshma asked him. "Amma?"

"No. Acchan," he replied, looking down.

"What did he do?"

"He is not my real father."

"Eh?"

It all came pouring out. In disjointed phrases interspersed with long pauses, he told her what his parents had told him that day. They had called him into the library and sat him down. Acchan had hugged him and said, no matter what he was about to tell him, he would continue to love him like he always had. Amma had tears in her eyes and silently mouthed the words, "I love you." It had filled him with a sense of impending dread. They told him that they had often thought about telling him what they were about to say, but had always concluded that it wasn't time yet.

"Enough already. Am I adopted? Just tell me!" he said.

Amma drew in a long breath and said, "No," before telling him everything.

*

Amma had just finished her PhD in sociology and had joined a university as an assistant professor. There, she had met and grown close to a colleague in the computer science department. He was much older than her and had a young son. He had been recently widowed and she was quite fond of the motherless boy. She moved in with them and hoped they could be a family together. But when she realised the man had no such intentions, she left. The disappointment of mismatched aspirations was hard. His refusal to stop her when she left felt as nonchalant as his reaction when she had moved in. The realisation that it had been an entirely one-sided affection was humiliating. What made matters worse was finding out she was pregnant. She had to quit her job and go home. She was too proud to seek his help. Her parents hadn't been very supportive, but her old college mate who had secretly been in love with her asked her to marry him when he found out about the baby. She accepted gratefully. Jacob had always thought of Juju as his own son and not once had he made her feel any different. Amma had insisted he take Jacob's name.

"Who is my biological father, then?"

"It's not important, darling. Anyway, I haven't seen him or heard from him since I left the university. He doesn't even know of your existence. I don't blame him. He didn't cheat me or anything. He never made any promises. He was just not available for us. But all that's pointless now. What counts is Acchan has been your father in every possible way; he has loved you with all his heart and we wanted you to know that."

"So what? You want me to be grateful for it?" he yelled.

"No, darling—"

He had stormed out of there in tears and kept walking until he reached Reshma's house. When he finished narrating his story, Reshma just looked at him and smiled. She looked just like she had when they were children, when his life had not been turned upside down by this new knowledge.

"Jacob uncle is very sweet," she said.

He wiped his tears and smiled back. She touched his shoulder, and he turned around to face her. He drew his breath in, and something happened to him. He sniffed again, as if to confirm something. And then he hugged her. She was surprised, but liked the feeling. He began visiting her regularly from then on. He had had sex education classes. She hadn't, but had seen a video on Daddy's phone that he had paused midway when he had gone for one of his rare baths. So she knew what was what.

Reshma and her friend began having sex, though neither of them spoke about it. It just happened and it felt right. While he had been affectionate and gentle around her body, it didn't seem as if he got anything out of it. He always stopped when she was done and didn't insist on going on. But that didn't deter him from coming to her, and he smiled and seemed at peace, so she assumed he liked it too. She felt as if she was borrowing his tools for her own chores. She accepted them gratefully, used them carefully and replaced them gently. And he was simply happy to lend them to her and revelled in her glow afterwards.

Mummy knew nothing about their little secret. When Reshma told her they needed a bigger receptacle for water, she simply spoke to Veena aunty and got their old blue barrel that stood unused in the backyard. It had earlier been used to replenish the lotus tank during the harsh summer months. But now that they had put a tap in the garden, all they needed was a hose for the job, and they were only too happy to let the dowdy old barrel go.

For a couple of years, their relationship remained undiscovered. Then, one day, just as abruptly as he had turned up, Juju stopped coming. Reshma waited for a few weeks before gathering her courage to go to Good Earth Community. Veena aunty was kindness itself. She received her in a flutter of nervous conversation. No, her Mummy wasn't there...she's usually in number twenty-two at this time of the day. Would she like a doughnut? She was having a little cheat day from her diet today...ha ha...she is amazed by Reshma's figure...what a sprightly young lady she has grown up to be! When she was her age, she had to struggle to keep the kilos off...

"Er...Aunty?"

"*Enni-ma?*"

"Ummm..."

"I know," she said lovingly. "You are here to ask after Juju. I know you're very close, and it breaks my heart to see you in pain. Trust me, child, I have been through the exact same thing, if not worse. This won't be easy for you, but you must make peace with it. Juju left for Delhi last week. He got a place at the most sought-after engineering college in the country. I thought he must have told you."

"He said he had taken the exam and was expecting to make it," Reshma said, as if in a daze.

"Yes. That private tuition did him the world of good. The poor kid has always been very talented, but couldn't realise his potential because of his dyslexia. Anyway, he had to rush to get his admission in before the deadline. His classes began right away, and he didn't have the time to say goodbye to any of his friends here. He hasn't even called home. You know how he is," Veena aunty said comfortingly.

"Yes, Aunty."

Veena aunty paused for a few seconds and looked down at the carpet at her feet as she spoke again. "Child, I think it's best if you forget him. He is whimsical…his emotions are unstable. You'll only set yourself up for more pain. I think he takes after his father." Something caught in her throat.

Reshma moved close and touched her knee. Veena aunty hugged her. They wept silently. Just then, Jacob uncle peeped in to ask if they'd like some tea. But, seeing them poised so poignantly, he left without saying a word. Veena aunty wiped her tears and smiled at her.

"You are a good child. Please take care of yourself. Jacob and I are here for you if you need us. Don't hesitate to ask us for any help, okay? Anything at all." She paused before continuing, "I heard there's a very nice fashion-designing course at the polytechnic. You'll need to have passed the SSC for it. Have you considered taking the external exam?"

"I'll think about it, Aunty," Reshma said, and rose to leave.

Veena aunty walked Reshma to the door and kissed her on the forehead.

"It's for your own good. Get over Juju."

It was hard to keep count of the years, as they were all identical in their hopelessness. In one of them, Reshma lost her job in the garment factory after she joined in the protests for better wages. Thanks to the time she had spent at school, she could read and write some English. She spoke confidently on the phone and could do basic arithmetic. She got small jobs here and there, enough for her to get by on, but none of these lasted for more than a few months.

A week had passed since she quit her job as a receptionist at a courier company, and she had been whiling away her time at home. Early that morning, long before sunrise, on a whim she picked up her phone and dialled his number. The call was cut in the middle of the second ring, but only a couple of minutes later her phone rang. He sounded a little tense, but not unhappy to hear from her. They spoke for a few minutes about mundane things, as if it hadn't been years since they spoke last. After he hung up, she just sat quietly for a long time.

When Mummy left for Good Earth Community that day, Reshma decided to make *burji* for Daddy and herself. Mummy would eat in one of the houses there and return in the evening with a packed dinner of assorted leftovers. Reshma was squatting on her haunches to peel an onion from the wire basket, when her senses were overwhelmed by her own smell. It was heady and musty, like soaked fenugreek seeds, and she felt a strong urge to masturbate.

She dropped the onions and walked to the little enclosure walled in by corrugated metal sheets that worked as a private bathroom. They only used it at night, as it had no roof and the neighbours could see in from the top of their concrete house. A family had moved into that house from the village a few years back, after selling their land. Their mule of a boy had flunked his SSC exams and had been making a nuisance of himself around the neighbourhood lately. There was talk that he had been beaten up for peeping inside someone's room, but that hadn't deterred him from his voyeuristic tendencies. She knew he would be hovering around the roof, hoping for a glimpse of someone in the bathroom, but today Reshma was beyond caring. It wasn't any latent exhibitionist instinct coming to the fore. She just wasn't bothered about privacy at that moment. She undid the drawstring of her *salwar* and sat down on the rough granite block that passed for a bathroom floor.

She returned to the room after a few minutes, wiping her eyes with the sleeve of her cotton kurta, and quickly dished out the *burji*. After Daddy and she ate it with *pao* – clutching the bread in their left hands and breaking pieces of it with their right to scoop up the *burji* mash from the pan – she cleared up the place and took the pan to the bathroom to be rinsed later. That's when she felt she must wash her hair. She felt grimy. Filthy.

She wasn't as agile as she used to be. She was also rather distracted that day as she waited for the water tanker to pass by. When it finally arrived, it did not stop for the signal at the side of the road, as usual, but a couple of scooters away, towards the middle. Reshma wriggled her way to it with the blue barrel, dodging bewildered motorists. She undid the valve with practised ease and the water gushed in. The sound of it falling into the hollow barrel was masked by the honking of impatient vehicles, as she had expected. The truck had only just come to a halt and there was a good two minutes before she would need to turn the valve off. But something strange happened. Reshma got all the water she needed to clean her hair in Juju's memory, but when the signal turned green and the truck began moving, she simply stood transfixed. She just stood there, staring ahead of her. Only when the horns blared and a scooter nearly knocked her over did she realise that the truck had moved ahead, and the water was still pouring out of the pipe. As if risen out of a deep slumber, she shook herself and ran after the tanker truck, abandoning her barrel. The truck turned at the signal and went left, with the gushing water leaving a dark trail on the dry tarmac. Her hair flew wild and her breasts jumped inside her loose kurta as she ran after the tanker, calling out to the driver to stop and turn the water off.

He saw her in the rear-view mirror and came to a screeching halt. He suddenly realised what had happened and rage filled his eyes. He jumped out of the truck and leapt for her throat. He grabbed her hard and, before she could react, he had struck her face with his open palm. "*Aramkor soolemagale!*" he screamed, as he rained blow after blow on her cheeks. "So, it's you who has been stealing the water from my tank all along?" He grabbed the neck of her kurta and ripped it all the way down to her waist, revealing an expensive but tattered underwired bra. He held her up by a fistful of hair as she was about to faint. "You nearly cost me my job, you whore," he yelled.

By then, the bystanders who had had enough of the morbid entertainment came to her rescue. "Leave her…she is not right in the head. Went to *inglis* school against everyone's advice. That's messed her up. Her mother is a poor woman who struggles to feed her family. Please let go…it's just a few buckets of water," they said, and got him to stop. Much water had flown from the tank under the bridge it was parked on. The driver shut the valve, salvaging what water he could for the deliveries he had ahead of him, before driving off, muttering aloud that he'd tear up more than just her shirt the next time he caught her. The crowd that had done its bit in freeing her from the vengeful hands of the tanker driver moved back and left Reshma alone as she slowly came to her senses and stood up.

Angry, palm-shaped welts were forming on her dusky cheeks. Her lip was cut and bleeding. Her left eye was swollen and was fast turning black. She gathered her torn kurta and held it up to her chest with one hand. She ran the other through her hair and smoothed over the knots as she dragged herself slowly back to her house. Tears mixed with kajal, blood and snot, forming melancholic watercolour strokes down her cheeks and her neck. Her heartbeat sounded to her like the rhythm she had learned in the rudimentary tabla class in that school she had attended as a child. How did it go? Dha – ge– na – te – na – ka – dhe – na. She stopped abruptly when she got home.

"Sujeeth?" she gasped. He had managed to drag the blue barrel to the tin shed from the road and was standing beside it, looking rather nervous. He looked at her and smiled weakly. Daddy walked out.

EIGHTEEN SPOONS

He blinked again, breathed in deeply and stared at the screen. The email marked "SP" didn't go bold. Disappointment didn't bother him anymore. A couple of years of regular rejection letters from publishers and literary agents had heightened his sense of equilibrium with "not-yet-ness" – a mild pang coupled with the propensity for renewed hope. But this seemed not to resemble not-yet-ness so much as the absolute end of the road. And that was indigestible. He did not know how to stop believing and this situation asked exactly that of him. Perhaps it was the switching of mediums that was causing the delay, he thought. A Facebook comment seeking an email in response or a hand-scribbled note seeking electronic acknowledgement usually takes longer than a response in the medium of the original message, he continued to reason with himself. His borderline-anxiety paranoia took over and he wondered if he had written something flippant to annoy her in the six or seven months since they had been communicating.

He knew he had always been proper and respectful in his emails – although the Facebook interaction had been slightly lacking in warmth owing to the town-square-esque nature of the platform. He loathed public displays of feelings – even shrouded ones. It was on Facebook that he had contacted her first. Anyone who was someone had a Facebook page these days, and it wasn't hard to tell between a fan page and a genuine profile. Hers was undoubtedly her own. He had sent her a personal message, written like a letter, with "Dear" and "Warm Regards", maintaining all boundaries. He had introduced himself, told her he admired her work, apologised for the intrusion on her time and had wondered if she might spare a moment to evaluate a story he had written. He had asked for her email address and had not been so presumptuous to send it to her on Facebook Messenger. Not once had he used the "wave" button that made an animated hand appear in the message box. He thought it disrespectful and silly, and unfriended anyone who used it with him.

She had responded politely – thanked him for trusting her with his unpublished work, said she was going to be busy all of that week, but promised to look at it soon and had asked for a reminder "if he didn't mind". She had also given him her personal email address. He had reminded her a week to the day later and she had written back with a two-page review for the five-page story, which was largely good, while noting that the characters seemed unnaturally symmetric – was he trying too hard? He was elated that she had noticed this subtle aspect and had responded gratefully, downplaying his excitement; nothing hid the thrill more than saying "I'm thrilled". Since then, they had communicated on and off over limited but concrete topics: him asking for publishing advice or book recommendations – things that she wouldn't have to go out of her way to give him.

She replied without much delay to each of his requests, gave adequate answers, and ended with a polite but obviously disinterested enquiry into his well-being. Neither one ever mentioned anything about their personal lives. Then, he had gone and shipped a copy of his first book of poems to her. He had not bothered asking her for her address and had sent it to the college where she taught creative writing. She hadn't responded.

Had something he had written in one of his emails angered her? Even that seemed like a desirable emotion, as opposed to the one he worried it could be (and was almost certain it was): apathy. Anger meant a mismatch of expectations, which meant she had had some to begin with, but apathy felt like a punch in the stomach.

Perhaps she had been busy? He checked her Facebook timeline and saw that there had been four posts in the last twelve hours – a new poem, a picture of her cat yawning, an impassioned denouncement of a regressive statement by a political leader and a witticism (*Avant-garde (defn): Highbrow absurd with a promise of depth subject to the audience's capacity to dig. #FilmFestivalofIndia*, which had received twenty-three "wows", forty-seven "laughs", eight "hearts", twelve "likes", and had been shared nine times). No, she had been online and active. So it was apathy, then. It was a reminder of an emptiness he had willingly ignored. Perhaps the joy he had sensed in her messages to him was a product of a wishful imagination; perhaps it wasn't anything more than an indiscriminate benevolence to strangers – all strangers. Perhaps he had never been special among strangers to her. Why would he be? There must be tens of people who wrote to her for literary advice every day. His inbox, visited every five minutes, remained as desolate as it had been forty-eight hours ago.

This was a new kind of rejection he had to teach himself to accept. He had toyed with the idea of telling her about his little train journey when he had visited his parents last week. Although the five-hour trip had been through a very picturesque landscape comprising rainforests, hills and waterfalls, he had travelled the route so many times that it had lost its novelty long ago. When he wasn't buried deep in a book, he absently observed his fellow passengers. Always shy to talk to strangers for fear one might turn out to be generous with small talk, he did venture gingerly into conversations when someone seemed kindly or sought some sort of help or took a sincere interest in his book. This woman told him she had gone to the city to seek medical help for her feet that had started to swell up suddenly the previous week. He had moved aside to give her room on his seat so she could rest her feet at an elevation to alleviate the swelling.

Having broken the ice thus, she had gone on to talk a little more. And, although she had asked him the usual questions about his salary and the number of children he had, his polite non-committal responses were not met with further inquisitiveness, as they normally were. Rather, she had turned the topic to herself. She had told him that her husband's brother's son also had a laptop like him and that he also read English books. Older women rarely refer to their husbands in the third person as "my husband". There's much awkwardness around the word. It's almost as if they are saying "the chap who bonks me", he had thought, and wondered if it would be too forward of him to say that in the mail he was planning to write her. They prefer to assume a relationship between the person they are talking to and the husband, to avoid the awkwardness of referencing their conjugality. He is either "your uncle" or "your brother", depending on their relative ages. But rather than "*nim unkul*", the lady with the swollen feet had surprised him by talking of her husband as "*nim* daddy". He had been amused and intrigued by it. He didn't know who he could talk to about it. Perhaps she would have liked to know?

But, two days later, he was glad he hadn't written to her about it – or anything at all. He liked the silence rather than the uninterested response of polite kindness that he was now convinced it would have elicited. He wondered if she would notice that he hadn't "liked" her posts in the last couple of days. Was he just one of the sixty to seventy likes her clever utterances got in the first hour of posting? His tendency for indecision was infamous. He had a habit of mentally reversing decisions he had made aloud earlier and forgetting to mention it to the people involved. This had cost him greatly in the past. He had been told to do something about it and he had spent sleepless nights over it to no avail. Now that he was alone, it didn't matter and he didn't stress over it anymore. But, strangely, this decision not to write to her held long enough for him to forget all about it.

It had been a good six months when the mail came. The subject line simply read *Eighteen spoons*. The mail body had this:

Eighteen spoons at once, unwashed
– and actions that followed –
In the sink are what it took to sink
Lower in his eyes:
So low that feet of crows
That rose for joy high by eyes
Were overrun with rivulets.
The method is gone and all that remains of the madness
Is itself.
I once walked on air
Several feet above worshipped ground
Nursing ethereal sparks waiting
To burst into words – refractive, ephemeral
Moaning meanings;
I peered absently at tax-return forms,
Cooked one-pot meals

And gave up driving as the roads demanded
Individual order in collective chaos;
I sat at the left window of the battered inheritance of a car
Smiling into the distance
And was called a hopeless navigator
Ever so tenderly that the smile stretched
To the outside reason.
But then, one after the other
The spoons sunk my reveries and stayed
Where I had left them – eighteen of them –
In the sink.

After this, almost as an afterthought, it simply read, *He hit me again last night.* Nothing more. The *Regards, SP* was a template signature. He could tell by the difference in the font.

He stared at it for a while and then got up to go for a jog. It had been weeks since he had gone jogging. When he did, it was with his earphones in place, playing the most unlikely exercise music – qawwali, thumri, Sufi songs on Coke Studio Pakistan, even classical bhajans.

"Are you not aware of the undisguised patriarchal basis of Vaishnavite literature?" she had asked him in disgusted surprise when she had curiously scrolled through his playlist. "Do you believe in that stuff?" she had demanded.

"I believe in the music. And the alliterative compositions soothe me," he had said.

It had been one of the many things. Even though it was a long time ago, he hadn't got over the habit of creating articulate justifications for his choices in his head.

Today, he didn't bother with the music. He jogged in silence. He ran past Anton's provisions shop; the sun was in his eyes and he waved in the direction he knew Anton would be sitting, relieved that there was no need for eye contact. He ran past houses with bottles of indigo-coloured water placed at their doorsteps to ward off stray dogs – a fad that had caught on like wildfire in the entire region, despite being proven to be a howling delusion, perhaps within an hour of the first pair of bottles being placed, when a dog must invariably have peed on one. He ran past the lake that was chock-a-block with lesser whistling ducks and lotus buds that looked like the logo on her bottles of perineal wash. He ran past little piles of burnt plastic garbage. There were PET bottles that had been burned even when they were half-full of water or sugary beverages. They had melted into amoebic shapes but remained sealed, transparent enclosures of liquid sitting in a pile of ash. He would normally be troubled by this, but today he didn't give them more than a distracted glance. He ran on air.

When he came back, there it was – the frenzied follow-up apology:

> I don't know what came over me. I'm not sure why I sent that mail to you. I just realised that having a room of one's own doesn't necessarily excuse one from housekeeping the others and thought you might understand. But we barely know each other, and the intimacy of the context must have bothered you. I cannot get away with blaming the wine. I apologise. Also, please don't judge my husband based on what I said (I really hope you can forget the whole thing). He is a good man. It's not gender. He has anger-management issues, and he is working on it.

The *Sincerely contrite* sign-off could not have been templated.

He didn't hit *reply* right away. Instead, he got up and began cleaning. The disorderly heap of stainless steel clanged as he pulled out one dish after the other from the sink. He squeezed a jet of watered-down soap out of the plastic bottle on to each dish, scrubbed until the lather frothed up, and rinsed them one by one under the tap. Whenever he washed a dish that had contained food with turmeric in it, he washed the yellow froth off the sponge and poured out fresh soap to wash the next vessel. He poured water over the lather that gathered over the drain and flushed the sink clean. He then wiped the kitchen counter with a rag. He arranged the books and stationery on his desk, dusted his bed and folded the sheets that had been lying in a pile for days. He changed the curtains and put the old ones in the washer. He swept, he mopped, he dusted, he vacuumed, he scrubbed the bathroom, he emptied the wet waste into the compost pit, he gathered up the dry waste into a garbage bag that claimed to be made of tapioca starch, to be taken to the municipal dumpster, from where it would eventually reach a landfill. He cleaned and cleaned until he was exhausted and floating on a mildly perfumed lilac cloud. He then stripped out of the sweatpants and pullover he had been wearing the last four days and took a cold shower. He dried himself with a fresh towel, dressed in a pair of clean cotton shorts with a red and grey checked pattern and a white T-shirt. He poured cheap red wine into a coffee mug (she had taken all the wine glasses with her) and carried it over to his desk. He opened his laptop and began typing.

Dear Sylvia,
That was a beautiful poem. Means a lot that you shared it with me.

(He hesitated a moment before continuing.)

> Please don't worry about writing to me what you did. That handful of mustard will not come from my house, nor can I cast the first stone – or any stone.

(He stopped to think and then wrote again.)

> Have you ever wondered how it is easy to say "my husband" in English, but not in an Indian language?

(Another pause.)

> Love,
> AR

THE AFTERLIFE OF TREES

T *he baobab is called the upside-down tree. When the leaves are shed, the bare branches resemble roots. The tree appears as if it has been planted in the intangible sky.*

The car's radiator had been acting up the last few days. The engine would overheat and cause jerky movements to the drive. The roadside mechanic who had attended to it had said the coolant was leaking. He had patched it up as best he could, but it needed attention at a company-authorised service centre. It looked like the car would have to be in the workshop for a week at least. The car owner couldn't afford to be separated from his car for that long. Also, the nearest city with that facility was not on his radar for at least a fortnight now. He was hoping he could contain the problem by driving slowly and taking more frequent breaks.

The car came to a complete halt in the middle of what seemed like nowhere. He opened the bonnet and the heat from the radiator sent him reeling back. He was out of water. He was also out of cash. He had meant to withdraw some money at the ATM near the dhaba where he had stopped for lunch. But his dog had got into a fight with a couple of local strays, and he had forgotten about everything else in trying to drag it back to the car. It was a hot afternoon and the highway mirage could have filled lakes. The earth was even and treeless and he could see for miles in all directions around him. He spotted what was possibly a little shop or a dhaba at some distance, but it wouldn't be less than a kilometre away. He let his dog out and it promptly peed on a rock nearby and sat panting, waiting to be given water. He stood there, hoping to flag down a passing vehicle and ask for water, but none stopped for him.

After it had been long enough for the light around him to feel so yellow it was brown, and his car so red it was black, he saw a figure emerge from the dancing waves on the road. At first, it looked like a large tree, its height diminished by distance, a symbol of itself in the never-ending aridness of the flat earth of childhood memories in an old continent. But it was moving towards him. When it came closer, he realised it was a man – a man walking with a wobbly gait, like he had corns on the soles of his feet. He was dressed in soiled clothes of a nondescript local style. He had a vacant expression on his face. As was the case with most village men, it was hard to tell his age. Weather beat their faces to look older than they were, but the physically challenging life they lived kept them fit enough to hide early geriatric signs. It was a double bind. He could have been anywhere between forty and sixty years old.

The man walked up to the car. Funnily, the dog that was always suspicious of strangers did not growl. It sniffed his crotch and wagged its tail, and the man patted its head. He asked the driver what the matter was, in the rustic Kannada of that region. When he found out that he needed water, he simply turned around and walked back the way he had come. He hobbled back soon with a one-litre plastic bottle of water. He said he had got it from a tap, but couldn't say more about where this mysterious tap and bottle had been found. He was speaking garbled words in incomplete half-sentences and it was difficult for the driver to understand most of what he said. He opened the radiator, which was still seething under the bonnet, and the water-bringer asked him to leave it open for a while and let it cool down a bit before pouring in the water.

"Too hot…water sudden…must not." He also reminded the driver to give some of it to his thirsty dog. The radiator hissed but didn't steam when he finally poured in the water. It seemed like the car was good for another short ride. The driver turned to the man who had helped him and asked him his name.

"I don't know, sir," he replied. "I carry a chit…pocket…write down. Today forgot…"

"Who writes it for you?"

"Home."

"Where do you live?"

He waved his hand in the general direction of the vast expanse beside the winding asphalt. "Village…there."

The driver couldn't see anything. "What do you do?" he persisted.

"Nothing now. Mechanic…before…accident."

"What accident?"

"Don't remember, sir."

The driver noticed that the man wore mismatched sandals that were barely intact. He offered him his own. "I am really grateful for your help. I wish I had some money to give you. Would you like to have my sandals? I see that yours are very old."

The man took one of his off and tried on the one that was offered to him. "Not like mine…slip."

The driver saw that the man's older ones had a toe grip, while his own had lateral straps that did not separate the toes. He realised the man was not used to wearing such sandals.

"Is there somewhere I can drop you? Take you back home perhaps?"

"No, sir. No, sir...I go." He slowly hobbled back in the direction from which he had come.

The car owner drove on the same stretch of road a few times that year. He stopped his car every time he passed the spot where he had had that breakdown, hoping to meet that nameless man who had helped him. He never saw him again.

*

Years had been spent on the road, constantly moving between points of rest. The red Ford Ikon, which had seen better days even before it passed many hands and reached Bhaubaab, was the means of motion. The will was his own. He had enough money to buy a brand-new car, but he didn't want to tempt fate with new things. Old things had something reassuring about them. They knew how to be used. They are worn even as they wear the hands that use them. And he wanted to fit into worn grooves rather than stick out, extraneously perched on solid, self-assured surfaces. Home, Bhaubaab had learned, was an ephemeral idea, and being settled in a place was settling for disillusionment and mediocrity. On the road, languages were his for the learning, food his for the eating. And experiences scrubbed his consciousness clean regularly. Rest could last from a day to a month – long enough to be replenishing and short enough not to disrupt the momentum of uprootedness. His desires were dispassionate, like dead wood. His thoughts of the future were clear without being definite.

While it was only a small portion – a sliver of sea-facing land – of a larger land mass jutting into the water that Bhaubaab claimed as home by right of generational memory, he realised that the rest of the country had also been rendered home by

126

historical political forces. As an overseas citizen, his Indianness had been stamped on papers, but he decided to do another translation of his status as *pravasi Bharatiya* and become a "travelling Indian", in which he'd assimilate the quality of Indianness as it came to him.

Such a precarious lifestyle could have been frowned upon, but he had no family to do the frowning. When at first he sold most of his larger possessions and brought down his belongings to what could fit into a couple of suitcases, the few friends he had told him he was being whimsical. It would pass. But they also wondered secretly if it would pass in time, as he had not been a young man in a while.

There had been no plan when he set out. He drove a hundred kilometres the first day, to a village where a couple he knew ran a school for the children of forest dwellers. He had run into them in the UK, years ago, when they were fundraising and his company had hosted them as part of its corporate social responsibility, and he thought them very nice. There had been a clampdown on foreign funding of independent social work such as this in recent years, and the couple was struggling to find teacher volunteers who would work without pay. They were very happy to have him help them out. "They are intelligent children. They learn everything so quickly – arithmetic, geography. But it's English that eludes them."

Children of all ages, dressed in rags of all descriptions, walked barefoot from their settlements in the forest every day to school. Bhaubaab did not know how to teach. But he knew how to be near people who valued earnestness and joy. The children were eager and curious, and when their inhibition about the newcomer broke, they began smiling at him. He started reading them stories from the library of donated books. At first, they suppressed giggles at his British accent. When they realised he was smiling back and wouldn't punish them, they giggled more openly. But, after a while, he realised their attention was waning, as "Scones with butter and honey for tea" and "going camping in the woods" first bewildered and then bored them. Not knowing what to do, he kept at it.

One day, a brawl broke out at the end of the class, in the middle of a story. One child had poked the other with something and she had bitten him in retaliation. Now they were on the floor, grabbing at each other's tufty hair. Bhaubaab broke up the fight and found that the first child had pricked the other one with a porcupine needle. He brought it to the front of the class and, between his passable Konkani and broken Kannada, asked them to describe the animal it came from. When they did, he translated it to English and, very slowly and clearly, said aloud, "Indian – crested – porcupine. It's a rodent – with a – coat of – spines." He made them repeat it. The children said it several times and were soon chanting it happily. One courageous child got up and started beating his feet to its rhythm. Soon, the rest joined in and the dance became a moving circle. "Indian crested porcupine. It's a rodent with a coat of spines," they yelled gleefully as they jumped and thumped around him. He stood there laughing and clapping until they tired themselves with the dance. That was his lesson for the day.

Stories and songs became the means of all education henceforth. The characters in them were drawn from the children, who fought among themselves to feature in that day's narration. Everyone got their turn. Bhaubaab built the plot as he went, and sometimes the children pitched in with twists and turns to it, based on what they thought they would do in the situations in which he put them. There were animals with magical powers, of course, and trees were sentient beings with the capacity for speech. He used the simplest of words possible and, when something beyond their limited English vocabulary was uttered, he stopped to explain the meaning and made them repeat it several times.

Little Manju was lost in a story. She had gone out to fetch firewood for her mother one evening when she saw a large butterfly – "A blue one with black border," as Somu said, "And with white lines like this, like this," as Babu claimed, and "White spots also," as Mahesh added – and, forgetting the wood, she went prancing behind it. It led her on a long chase, flitting from flower to flower, from branch to branch, never letting her lose sight of it, always a little out of reach. Soon, dusk descended on the world and Manju couldn't tell where she was. She didn't know her way back, as everything looked unfamiliar. Trees swaying in the wind seemed like witches waving and calling out to her to enter their mouths. Owls hooted eerily, hawks screeched and jackals howled in the distance. She was so scared, she couldn't walk anymore. She sat down on a fallen tree trunk and wept. She heard loud thunder.

"Do you know what happened then?" Bhaubaab asked.

"It began raining?"

"Yes! It began raining so hard that Manju was drenched right away. She missed her mother and brother and wanted to be home in the warmth of her kitchen eating hot gruel—"

"And dried fish?"

"And dried fish. Just then, she saw a light coming towards her from afar. She could hear footsteps. *Thud, thud, thud.*"

Suddenly, Shobha let out a shrill scream and began crying.

"No, no, don't cry. It's all going to be fine. Everything will be all right. It has a happy ending. It always ends happily. Just listen on."

Everyone turned to Shobha and hurriedly assured her that there would indeed be a happy ending – to make her stop crying, so they could hear the rest of the story. Bhaubaab put Shobha on his lap and comforted her before continuing.

"The light turned out to be the torch in the hands of Adavi-amma, the kindly forest goddess who lived deep in the jungle and appeared only to good girls and boys. She wore a green sari made of leaves, and had flowers in her long hair. Her face was kind and her smile sweet. "Shhh…child, I won't hurt you. I'm here to help you," she said, and Manju stopped crying. Adavi-amma hugged Manju and rocked her gently. She took Manju to her house and gave her dry clothes."

"A yellow frock?"

"Yes, a yellow frock, and nice things to eat…Bananas, mangoes…"

"Cream biscuits?"

"Cream biscuits…"

"Maggi?"

"What? How…? Er…okay, Maggi too."

"Coca-Cola?"

"No, Salvador, Coca-Cola is bad for you. Stop grumbling! She let her sleep on a soft bed. She gave her many gifts for her brother and her parents, and sent her back home the next morning riding on a deer's back. The deer dropped her right in front of her house and vanished. When Manju showed her new dress and the gifts she had brought to her brother, he was overjoyed. He wanted to know who gave them to her, but Manju simply said she got them from the forest. When their mother came home from work and saw the gifts, she winked at Manju and said, 'I know who gave them to you.'"

"How did she know?" the children wanted to know.

"That's another story. I'll tell you tomorrow," Bhaubaab said.

*

It had been several months, now. The children could form small sentences in English, and they were more confident in their reading. But Bhaubaab was beginning to look a little morose. When his hosts asked him if everything was all right, he said he worried he was beginning to get attached to the children. That was the one thing he wanted to avoid at all costs. When he told them that he wanted to leave, they were sad but understanding. He promised them he'd return every year to tell stories to the children.

He travelled around the country, driving on the highway to gain distance before turning off into side roads and dirt tracks to seek destinations. He taught in village schools; he helped fix tractors, tillers and other farm equipment; he rescued people and snakes from each other; he stayed in farm sheds, in the homes of people who extended impromptu invitations, in bus shelters, in the open when the weather was fine; he slept in his car when he couldn't find anything and treated himself to an occasional hotel room when he felt that his aging body needed a break from the hard life. He ate in roadside *dhabas* and small tea shops. He ate food cooked on open fires in fields with the farmhands; he ate special food cooked in his honour in the homes of his hosts for the day; he bought himself burgers at McDonalds on the highway. He had picked up a puppy he found sitting beside its road-kill mother one day. Having chewed his car seats to shreds over the months, it was now a full-grown dog and his travel companion. Bhaubaab often spoke aloud to it while he drove. His roots were up in the air and his spirits were high.

He returned to the school every year to teach English. He had no illusions about it making a particularly big difference. These were children of the forest. They traced their roots back to Africa through many, many stories of love and loss. They looked very dissimilar to mainland people. They stood out and were kept on the margins. The little English they learned was just enough to show them that there was a world outside of their own – a big, shiny, colourful world, with fascinating things to see and do – a world they couldn't be a part of. Even if they ventured out, they could only see, but not touch. They could learn that their forest home was being taken away from them a little at a time, but they didn't have the means to save it. They couldn't go back to doing what their parents did, and they couldn't do city things or live city lives. The crafts and little technical education they got in the school would keep them just alive enough to grow unhappy and cynical. Bhaubaab did not worry himself too much with these concerns, however. He was self-sufficient in this journey of asking no bigger questions. His stories brought momentary joy to the children and that was enough for him.

It was a dark, rainy evening when his car broke down. The battery had been giving him some trouble and he had been postponing a visit to the mechanic. Because of that, his flashlight and phone weren't charged either. The nearest village was an hour away on foot. Fortunately, he had enough food and water for the night, for himself and his dog. The drizzle turned into a downpour suddenly. He wound up the windows and got ready to call it a night. If he was worried that there had been a lynching incident in that area a week ago, when two men in

Rastafarian caps who had stopped their car for a smoke had been beaten to death by a mob on suspicion of being kidnappers, he did not dwell too much on it. He was tired from the drive, and he fell asleep quickly.

He was woken up by the barking of his dog around midnight. He saw a light approaching his car from a distance.

A CAT NAMED INSOMNIA

I'm a computer program. I'm zipping in permutations of green bits manifesting across real distances through ethereal mediums. I make small, semiconducting blipping sounds. I'm a little boy with vitiligo – receding pigments forming maps on my skin, my colour causes tectonic shifts. I wear continents like underwear. I lack the memory to look wistful over the loss of cities as pensioners' paradises. They are to me what they are: smoggy, boggy, reclaimed lakebeds bloated with plastic and lies – their history, an elite pastime. Who was it who said the child is father of the man? I have a cat named Insomnia. She is a calico. I cannot sleep.

I cannot sleep. I haven't slept since the day my son was born; the day my wife died. She didn't die in childbirth. She drowned in the bathtub. My son was saved by a whisker. She entered the water clutching him to her breast. The nurses pulled him out of her grasp. Perhaps it was because he had not long been out of amniotic fluids that my son felt at home in the bath water and didn't thrash about or take any in his lungs, and lasted the time it took for the nurses to rush to his rescue. I don't know. I was there, but I remember nothing of it. I was immobile, they said. I was just kneeling on the floor and weeping uncontrollably, they said. Perhaps they didn't expect her to be taking her own life. Perhaps they assumed she simply wanted to ease the pain of childbirth in a warm bath and was too dazed to remember to keep the baby out of harm. They let her be as soon as they pulled the baby out and got busy attending to him. She just sank into the water and died. It all happened so fast, everything that was said about it was mere retrospective speculation.

Finally, they attributed it to postpartum depression and closed the "case". A doctor who had known her longer said it could have been schizophrenia. But I think all that is just a way of putting labels on things that cannot be known – paying obeisance to the end of human knowledge, defining from the outside the dark, mysterious spaces of human minds that cannot be breached. Like death. Like God. I know what it was with her – only, I cannot explain it without having a label thrust on me too.

I came home with my newborn son. A son I did not want, one I had vehemently not planned on having. A son who became my whole life. My saviour. At first, I did not know what to do with him, but memories of rescuing cats and dogs and little birds came back, and I rose to the occasion. I taught myself how to mix his formula to the right consistency, how to test the temperature of the bathwater with my elbow, how to hold him on one arm while I bathed him with the other, how to clean him and change his diaper, how to hold and comfort him when he cried, all of it. The Internet was a big help, of course. Detailed videos on every child-rearing challenge were a blessing. I missed his mother terribly, but there was simply no time to feel sad. Also, after what had been and what we had gone through since the time he was conceived, despite myself, I felt that her absence was something of a relief.

The university was most understanding about my situation. They allowed me to forgo all master's programme classes and I only had a handful of my research students to attend to, who were happy to meet me at home instead of my office. They came when my son slept in the afternoons, and spoke in hushed tones.

On days that I had to go to the office for some nominal work or other, I carried him with me in a swaddle sling. My colleagues sympathised with me and fawned over my son. I had been raised by a single father myself; I knew I could do this.

I named him Bassam, which meant "one who smiles" in Arabic. I wanted him to be shielded from what I had been through and hoped that perhaps his name might be more successful in cheating fate than mine had been. Also, I didn't want his name to be tied to a religion. Even though his mother and I had been staunchly anti-religious, our names hadn't been particularly innocent of factions. Bassam was Arabic, but not a popular Muslim name in this part of the world. I wouldn't want to sling a label on my son that would prove to be a sentence if he was stuck in the wrong place at the wrong time, would I?

I immersed myself in his care, but, in all this, I had become a heavy insomniac. In the initial months after my son's birth, he kept me up all night. He did not cry much, but it was my own subconscious that told me I had to do the job of two that made me stay up to attend to him. The sleeplessness just stayed with me. I would doze off for a few minutes before I'd be woken up by strange dreams. Nights felt like a constant psychedelic trip, and not a happy one. The fatigue caught me every now and then, and I would slip into an hour or so of unconsciousness – not sure if I can call that sleep – every two days or so. And that's how I managed to stay alive. I lacked energy and enthusiasm in everything. The only thing that kept me going was the pressing need to be there for Bassam.

Despite my constant forlornness, Bassam grew up to be a happy child. He was healthy, intelligent, funny and physically active. But, most importantly, he was kind and respectful. He began attending the Kendriya Vidyalaya on the university campus. He was a great hit among his friends, and their natural leader.

Bassam must have been around thirteen when that neon green line of resilience in my bones, which had stretched and stretched till its ductility, snapped. I was in my study, nursing my third small bourbon with a colleague from the department of astrology who had dropped by to chew the fat after dinner. As a man of science, I should have perhaps joined my colleagues in resisting the inclusion of irrational subjects at the university when it was started a few years ago, but I had a baby son to look after and couldn't afford to wave at the changing tide.

He was talking passionately about the city's deterioration in recent years. "It's going to the dogs, I tell you. I was in London for a conference last year and what roads those buggers have... such amazing roads, *yaar*. You can sleep on them. Our city used to be like that, once upon a time. I remember my grandfather taking me for walks in the cantonment area...*pchah!* What magnificent buildings...What stately cars...The roads lined with trees. Now, you couldn't find a hint of the bygone era if you searched with a torch. It's only traffic and garbage, traffic and rubbish...no civic sense only. It's all this IT crowd, I tell you. They descend upon the city like locusts and ruin its culture. If this continues, there's simply no telling what will happen to my beloved city. There's simply no te—"

"Sorry, *yaar*. I have got to go," I said, and put my glass down.

"Go? Go where?"

"I don't know. I just need to go."

"What? Is everything okay?"

I didn't bother to wait and answer his questions. I just went to my bedroom and began packing.

Bassam walked in and saw me in a frenzy, stuffing things into my suitcase. But instead of asking me what I was doing, he simply reminded me of the essentials I should take – my toiletries, socks and underwear, phone charger, e-reader, wallet with all the cards, etc. – and helped me pack. There was a strange, reassuring quietude about him. He seemed almost thrice as mature as one would expect for his age. Not only had he been looking after himself, but he had also been a great emotional crutch for me. I'm not sure when that happened, but I had, without realising it, come to lean on my son a lot of late. I looked at him helplessly.

"Don't worry about me, Appa," he said, "I'll be fine. You'll be back soon, anyway."

How did he know that? I didn't ask him. We had a regular cook now and a lady who came in three times a week to clean. The larder was stocked up for two weeks. There were no outstanding bills for the utilities. Bassam did his schoolwork without being asked and he had his books and friends to keep him occupied. The university campus was a safe place, and my colleagues and neighbours would help in an emergency.

I picked my bag up and left. I caught a train to the hills. What I did there is unimportant, as I did mundane, touristy things: stayed in a hotel, checked out the sights, sampled local cuisine, went for walks, read, slept. It is all hazy now. I returned after a week. Bassam was happy to see me, in his usual, calm way. I was happy to see him too, but I wanted to go again.

I once saw a woman chased by a swarm of bees. She had been walking under a tree on whose boughs hung very large hives, and some mischievous neighbourhood boys had pelted them with stones. The poor, unsuspecting woman was walking under it with a pile of wood on her head when they came after her with misplaced vengeance. She dropped the wood and ran for her life. The bees engulfed her in a matter of seconds, and she must have been stung a few hundred times. The fiery pain must have been overwhelming, but she just didn't stop running. I don't think it helped ease the pain. The instinct not to stop must be connected to the fear of fighting the pain. You run and you run. The pain goes with you, but your legs are busy, so you have an excuse to not face it. They had to tackle her down to the ground to help her. They threw large, burlap sacks soaked in water on her, to beat out the bees before she could be treated. Even then, she kept rolling on the ground and wouldn't hold still. I think I know why I was reminded of her then.

I had been invited for a seminar at a foreign university earlier that month. I accepted this one, though I'd refused all such offers in the past. Soon after I came back, I left for a conference in another country. Seminars, conferences, workshops and meetings followed one after the other. If nothing else, I was invited to be part of juries for research theses. As a highly respected botanist, grants, fellowships and residencies were available to me for the asking. When it couldn't be official, I took a sabbatical from the university and travelled.

Any country with any semblance of a university in it was a potential destination. My returns were little more than laundry stops. Jetlag blended seamlessly with my insomnia and the rest I got in transit felt adequate. In fact, I slept better on planes: perhaps the knowledge that I was with dozens of people who sat facing in the same direction, hurtling with the same velocity through the sky towards the same destination as me, and whose lives, like mine, for the next few hours would be in the hands of two or three chosen people, was more lulling than anything else had been in years. Not having control felt good. Being airborne was like being tackled to the ground with soaking burlap sacks to beat out the bees swarming me. I ran with a rhythm beating in my ears like it was a whispered secret, or a deceptive lie. Dha – ge – na – te – na – ka – dhe– na. I ran and ran through every possible continent, every kind of geography, until it stung less.

When I finally returned, travel weary, sunburnt – or frostbitten – Bassam was a young adult. He had turned into a handsome twenty-year-old who reminded me of my father. He was in college now, studying foreign policy or some such. I vaguely remembered handling his admission formalities on one of my visits home. He welcomed me back like an old friend. Although our relationship had become something else altogether, it didn't feel strange to be cohabiting with him afresh. We settled into a routine. We ate breakfast together every morning, after which he would leave for college, and I for my office, each with a packed lunch. We met again at dinner time. We spoke when we felt like it, but were otherwise very comfortable to sit in silence in each other's presence. We shared aftershave.

One day, Bassam came home with a kitten. A tiny little calico. It hadn't opened its eyes yet. He said it was born in his friend's house. It was the runt of the litter and the mother had attempted to eat it. His friend had stopped that from happening, but when he tried putting the kitten back in with the rest of its siblings, the mother had forsaken it. Since he feared the mother would eat it if left unsupervised, he had given it to Bassam to raise. I was sceptical about it. It was too young to survive without a mother.

"Are you sure you mean that, Appa?" he said, cocking one eyebrow up.

I felt like an idiot. Also, something stirred in my heart and I thought of my last cat – Bassam had been conceived on the day it died.

"I can't tell if it's a boy or a girl," Bassam said, holding the kitten out to me in one hand.

"It is a girl," I said, taking the kitten in my cupped hand, but not bothering to turn it over and check.

"How can you be so sure?" Bassam's thick eyebrows came together.

"It's a calico. Calicos are always female."

"How?"

"It is only the X chromosome that can have the locus of the orange gene. Y doesn't. You need both XXs – one with orange and one without – to bring out the pattern. Wikipedia stuff, really," I said, trying to downplay my pleasure at the admiring look in my son's eyes with modesty.

*

Together, we began caring for the kitten. I found an old electric heating pad that my late wife had used to ease her menstrual pain. To my surprise and joy, it still worked. We placed the kitten on it, wrapped in a fleece blanket to keep it warm. At the pet store, we bought kitten formula and a tiny nipple that would fit its mouth, and we took turns feeding it. In the absence of the mother's tongue, Bassam held an old towel between his fingers and rubbed the kitten's genitals gently to stimulate urine. We cleaned its litter box every time it pooped or peed. We kept it warm and dry at all times and the kitten survived.

It had a very interesting colour pattern. While it was mostly white and orange all over, with only a few small black patches near its rump, it had two very distinct black half-moons under its eyes – like a child that had laid its hands on its mother's kohl. "She looks like you," Bassam teased me, and named her Insomnia. When Insomnia was old enough to eat solid food, the vet asked us to feed her fresh food and to avoid store-bought cat food. Kibble is all right for emergencies or as a treat once in a while, but its constant use could cause kidney problems in her old age. Give her fish and avoid milk products, we were told. That put me in a bit of a fix. I had been raised a vegetarian. I had briefly taken to eating non-vegetarian food with my wife, but had gone back to being vegetarian after her death. I had raised Bassam as one too. I didn't know how to shop for fish. But Bassam seemed to know exactly what to do. The boy never ceased to surprise me.

We marched down to the fish market. It was a large shed with long cement counters on which people exhibited their wares, calling out to customers in shrill tones. The floor was wet and the air was heavy with the smell of fish and sounds of haggling. Cats of all descriptions walked around looking for a quick bite. I felt lost in that place and simply followed Bassam, who led the way through the counters. He stopped before a woman at the end of the line.

Her wares were nondescript – they were fish of various kinds, just like everyone else's. But there was something strange about the woman. She stood out from the rest. While most of them were buxom, homely figures dressed in cheap saris pulled up to their knees, their hair in buns with flowers around them, this woman was thin and tall and was dressed in a worn and faded, but beautifully fitting, Khaadi kurta and jeans. Although grimy, her loose hair seemed to hark back to a better-groomed time. She wore round glasses. She spoke English. She looked a few years younger than me, though how many I couldn't tell. I wondered if she was put there as part of a reality TV show, if her fish were booby trapped, if someone would jump out from behind the wall if we bought from her and shout that we had been pranked and would now appear on some silly web series that no one watched. But, going by the way she interacted with her fellow fishmongers and customers, she seemed genuine all right. Her appearance apart, the most interesting thing about her was a peculiar body odour. People who handle fish aren't exactly easy on the nose. Nor are individual scents easy to tell in a fish market. But hers hung in a thick olfactory aura around her. I couldn't quite place it. It reminded me of something deep and rank, like fermenting batter, forgotten for weeks. It was far from pleasant. I kept myself from retching out of politeness. After asking about slices of seer fish, pomfret and mackerel, Bassam bought a handful of sardines from her. If she was disappointed or irritated by it, she didn't show it. I simply stood back, watching the exchange between them. I know my son is a respectful young man, but his attitude to her was almost as if she were royalty. It was also strangely tender. When we walked back, I asked him what that was all about. He shrugged and didn't encourage further questioning.

We bought fish from the same lady every week. Initially, Bassam and I went together, then he stopped coming and I began to do the fish shopping by myself. In a month's time, I had discovered her name and the fact that she had had a few years of schooling. Also, that she had moved to this part of the city a few years ago. It was after about six months that Meena blurted out that she didn't take baths. I didn't know how to react to that and surprised myself by assuring her that I didn't mind. She gazed at me without comment, her expression not changing. It was another month later that she asked me if I had *Blackadder*. A snake? What? It took me a minute to remember the BBC pseudo-historical sitcom from the 1980s. How did she know of it? She told me that she had seen it in the house of some uncle and aunty of hers. I was even more intrigued. I told her I didn't have it, but I could download it for her if she liked.

Meena visited our home in the evening, the next weekend. She didn't seem confused or out of place in our mellowly lit drawing room. Bassam was very happy to see her and made us a chickpea salad with tomatoes, onions and coriander, dressed with lemon and pepper, to munch on while we watched the show. I sat across from her, trying not to breathe too deeply. But, despite her stench, I was drawn to her.

One day, as Bassam and I sat sipping black coffee at breakfast, he suddenly looked up from his book and said, "You should get married again."

"Don't be silly. She will never agree," I said, without looking up from my iPad. I immediately realised what I had just said and looked up.

His eyes were already there waiting to meet mine. His arms were folded across his chest and his head was cocked to one side, while a small smile played on his lips.

"I mean…I…well…" As I stuttered, he burst out laughing.

"I think she will," he said, and left for college.

That evening, Meena arrived at my home without ceremony. Bassam was staying over with a friend, and I didn't know what to say to her. I asked her in and made her a cup of tea. She asked me if she could take a shower. I showed her the bathroom and found her a towel. I hadn't thought about anyone sexually since my wife died. I had been a full-time father and a fugitive academic; a chronic insomniac on the run – running and running from an unknown assailant, not stopping to see who or what it was. I had probably also been unconsciously loyal to my late wife, thinking of intimate companionships as cheating on her memory.

While Meena was in the bathroom, I texted Bassam to tell him she was there.

Appa, water washes, water fluxes. Amma would understand, he replied. This was followed by another text telling me he wouldn't be back until late afternoon the next day.

Meena came out of the bathroom after three quarters of an hour, wrapped in the towel I had given her. Her wet hair hung limp against her shoulder. Her skin was scrubbed pink. She smiled at me shyly. She followed me into my bedroom. Her characteristic odour felt like it had been scoured clean, leaving behind the most enticing of smells. It had lost its mouldy, fermenting overtones and instead there was a fresh, soothing muskiness. I hugged her and was instantly reminded of deep dark kitchens in old mud houses, of freshly laundered linen, wood fires, rows and rows of glass jars containing herbs and seeds, arranged on low shelves, of *dosas* sizzling on cast-iron pans, of lemon trees in the backyard. She smelled like a potpourri of caresses, and smiles through tears.

We lay down on the bed and I instantly fell into a cavernous black slumber in her arms. I felt like I had been asleep for years when I woke up the next morning. I felt quenched. That feeling, although vaguely familiar, was not one I'd had in eons. She was there beside me, with one arm over my shoulder, wide awake and smiling. We made love. While my late wife and I had had our lustful moments in bed, it felt different with Meena. She knew exactly what she wanted and how to get it. She directed me and moved me and took charge of my body with uncanny ease. I was rusty and was relieved to let her lead the way. After we were done, I lay back and cried. I felt awash with so many forgotten sensations. I hadn't cried or slept deeply since the day Bassam was born. I felt thawed.

I had a hundred questions I wanted to ask her. Where did she come from? Who was in her family? Where did she live? Why did she come to me? But somehow those questions seemed to have evaporated from my head like the thick insomniac clouds, and I felt cured of my curiosity. Then she, of her own volition, told me that her name wasn't actually Meena. There had been a spate of name changes on campus around the time the astrology department was started. Our housekeeper Chandbi, for instance, had started calling herself Chandramma, and she was mighty touchy about it. I didn't want to embarrass Meena by asking her what her original name was. Instead, I asked her if I could continue to call her Meena, and she said yes. I left it at that.

When Bassam came home later, Meena and I were lounging on the sofa, watching reruns of *Blackadder* and drinking tea. He came in grinning widely and winked at me. I blushed.

Meena looked at him warmly and said, "I don't want to lose home again."

I didn't know what she was talking about. But Bassam assured her that she would never have to do that.

"What about you? You will want the house, no?" she asked him.

"Don't worry about me. I have other plans," he said.

I got nothing of that exchange, but, by then, I had stopped trying. Bassam went abroad for his master's degree. Meena and I have been married a year now. My insomnia is cured, and our cat is spayed.

A CAT NAMED INSOMNIA

I bought a plot of land to build a house. It is beside the fifty-acre ashram of Guru Nine-Finger Narayana. The place is perfect. It is not so close to the city that the noise and pollution would affect us, and not so far that we cannot access its amenities. The god-man has ensured that the area is green and wooded, and thanks to his disciples among the who's-who of the what's-what in the administration, the place will never want for civic comforts. The road leading up to it was built and maintained under express order in the Asphalt Diamond project. The water supply is flawless, there is no electric outage and the Internet is faster than anywhere else. The soft-spoken, new-age guru with impeccable English and handsome looks is a great hit with the younger generation of professionals and entrepreneurs. He holds forth on everything – social, cultural or metaphysical – in a steady, non-bombastic manner. His theory of the ethical pursuit of pleasure as the way to fulfilment draws disciples by the thousands every day from all over the world. They are by order an orderly lot and I don't worry about loud chants or mountains of trash.

I ventured into one of his sermons one day, purely out of curiosity, and disciple volunteers ushered me in with the politest of smiles. He was saying something to the effect of opposable digits being just a physical manifestation of the cosmic capability of the human mind, and that we are limited in the attainment of *shoonya* by concentrating purely on the physical. He was calling for his followers to transcend the complacency of our physical capabilities to seek oneness of the soul with the centre of the universe – he claimed to have shed one of his thumbs by divine ordinance to prove this theory in person. That serene calmness of his demeanour did, in fact, seem like the picture of utmost fulfilment. He prescribed his "non-digital" meditation technique for this purpose, and everyone was shedding tears of enlightenment. I couldn't care less for all this bunkum, but Meena loved the range of "healing" scented candles in the ashram shop – particularly the large ones called "Fresh Linen".

Meena wants a rammed-earth house with a central courtyard and a large bathroom with a blue bathtub. I want her to have what she wants. Sometimes I wonder what everything was all about. But I just smile and go back to sleep.

R.I.P.

All rest and all peace is for the living
Know peace while you can
What if what lies beyond is more of the same thing?
Get some sleep tonight

She hadn't planned on walking both ways. Although Kumily wasn't hot even during the peak of summer, walking twelve kilometres – six of which were uphill – had been exhausting.

Sylvia had, at first, rejoiced that her hostess and teacher was a reticent woman who would not compel her to talk and share her story, but, in the two months she had spent there as an art apprentice, she had become a little edgy about the lack of words her new life entailed. Since her last break-up a year ago, she had been facing a staggering writer's block that showed no sign of thawing. Professional jealousy had been the root cause of the break-up, according to her therapist, and she hadn't been able to grapple with the profoundness of it. She also worried that the escitalopram and aripiprazole she had been on for the past couple of years had, in the guise of stabilising her moods, cemented in the cracks of her mind, sealing in the springs of kaleidoscopic imagination. She loved nothing, she hated nothing, and her thoughts did not transcend the then and the now.

That's when she sought to experiment with other ways of expression that would perhaps help her find her voice again. When she had approached the famous artist with a reputation for being a recluse, to seek her tutelage, she had refused flatly, saying art could not be taught. But Sylvia had persisted until the woman finally relented and said she could watch her at work so long as she didn't utter a word while she painted. Sylvia could stay in the spare room in her large, rather desolate, bungalow and do her own cooking. She would comment on Sylvia's work only when she felt like it, which wasn't often.

One day, on a whim, she had stopped her medication without asking her doctor. The thaw came. It came as vivid, chimeric dreams; as crying spells that lasted hours; as numbing headaches that demanded shut-eyed nursing in the foetal position. But, on days when the headaches eased, she went in search of interesting images of quotidian Kumilyness – which wasn't very different from a general highland Keralaness – to spin a pun around or write an acerbic paragraph about. She posted these on Facebook, and the congratulatory comments lifted her spirits. The other day, she had been in an auto when she spotted a curious shop board. *Hijab Attar Sent*, it read. She knew the misspelt words would make for a funny post, but she couldn't take a picture while in the autorickshaw and decided she would walk back to the place the next morning.

But, the next day, she forgot the exact location of the shop and walked all the way to the KSRTC bus stand without finding it. All along, she worded and reworded the post in her head. She even fantasised about which of her friends would have equally funny responses to it. When she realised she had probably passed the spot without noticing, she decided to walk back looking for it, rather than take an autorickshaw, as she had planned on doing. To her dismay, the shop turned out to be right at the corner, not even five minutes from where she lived. She'd missed it earlier because there had been a truck parked in front of it when she passed by.

She was tired and sweaty when she returned home, making straight for her room. Her teacher would be applying her first washes for a new painting. There wasn't much to learn in that and, in fact, it had begun mattering less and less. The cold air dried her sweat as soon as she stopped walking and gave her a chill. She wrapped a shawl around her shoulders and sat down at her laptop. She quickly cropped the image of the shop board, focusing on the words, masked the phone number on it, adjusted its colour saturation and contrast, and posted it with the words she had been practising all day. She had just sat back, waiting for the comments to begin appearing, when she got a message on WhatsApp. A friend's father had died.

They hadn't communicated in a while, but Sylvia liked her. Why had she let that bloody Sujeeth treat her like that? Sylvia had wondered often, but hadn't said anything to her. (Relationships are so fucking complicated, *ya*...Who the hell am I to judge someone for doing things differently? It's not as if I'm particularly successful in loving or being loved myself.) She wanted to reach out to her. She opened a fresh email and began typing. *Dear,* she wrote and paused. After the last Facebook post, she was feeling creatively exhausted and didn't know how to mitigate the emptiness of formality. She tried putting herself in her friend's place. If she received a letter of condolence upon her father's death, how would she react? *Thank you. We weren't close,* she'd say. It was not just the lack of closeness – in the vitriol she had felt for him at first, any bitterness she might have had had also burned itself out, leaving a passionless emptiness. She had made her peace with his absence long ago. And that's how her polite rejection of the weepy old man's attempts to make peace had been so remorseless. *We weren't close*, was in fact overkill for a reminder of a long-forgotten lack.

She shut her laptop, pulled out her phone from her pocket and wrote her friend a text message. *Hey, I can't imagine what you must be going through. I actually can't. But if you want to talk, I'll be happy to* – she deleted the last four words; *happy* wasn't a word you used on a sombre occasion like this – *I can listen*, she typed. *I'm returning in a couple of days. Let me know if you want to come home. There'll be beer. I'll cook.* She hit *send* and lay back on her bed. She suddenly felt very homesick.

Perhaps I should go back to one of my many unfinished works. Maybe that would push me through the block, she thought. Just then, her agent called. She had told him not to disturb her unless it was something very pressing.

"Sylvia! I got a call from someone asking for you. He found out from my website that I represent you. Bugger wouldn't stop insisting on getting in touch with you. Was saying something about a memoir. Had a funny-sounding name…Sagittarian, or something…"

"Cajetan? I hope you saved his number."

She had been getting her thyroid tested every year since Mama was diagnosed with hypothyroidism. But it was always "normal". Everything was normal. Her prandial grandiose, that night, was in celebration, however. She ate three aloo parathas drenched in butter, with tamarind and jaggery chutney, seasoned with red chillies and cumin, and a side of roast-chicken salad with hollandaise sauce. She had a scoop of ice cream with a hunk of the plum cake left over from breakfast, and promised herself she would begin a diet the next week. She turned the lights off, lit a red pillar candle and poured herself a glass of the dessert wine she had put away the last time she had stopped drinking. She drank the rest straight from the bottle and took her aripiprazole. She was smiling to herself when she went to bed. She was to head home the next day.

GLOSSARY

Term	Language	Explanation
aan-de...sob haram khoran-ku maar'k sata-toon	Dakhani Urdu	Let them come... the bastards...I'll slay them!
abbu	Urdu	Father
acchan	Malayalam	Father
acharya	Sanskrit	Brahmin priest
Afrikar	Konkani	People of Goan origin living in Africa
akka	Kannada	Older sister
Amar Chitra Katha	Proper noun	A comic book company that popularised stories from Indian mythology among children and young adults
amchem	Konkani	Our
amma	All south Indian languages	Mother
anna	Kannada	Older brother
appa	Kannada, Tamil	Father

aradhani	Kannada	Worship ceremony of the reigning deity
aramkor soolemagale	Kannada	Bastard daughter of a whore
Awo bhabhi, kya hona?	Dakhani Urdu	Come, my sister-in-law. What will it be today?
Bamon	Konkani variation of Brahmin	Highest of the four varnas of the Hindu social order in India.
Banajiga	Proper noun	A Kannada-speaking mercantile caste belonging to the Lingayat denomination
bayst	Konkani	Corruption of "best"
beedi	Most Indian languages	Country cigarette
Bharatiya	All Indian languages	Indian
Bunt	Proper noun	An Indian community originally from the coastal districts of Karnataka

burji	Hindi	Spicy scrambled egg
dhaba	Hindi	Roadside restaurants in India
doce de grao	Portuguese	A Goan sweet preparation made of chickpeas and sugar
dodda hunasemara	Kannada	Large tamarind tree
dosa	Noun	Rice batter pancake
durbar	Persian-derived	A king's court; holding court
enni-ma?	Tamil	Yes, my dear?
feni	Noun	Liquor popular in Goa. Typically available in two variants: cashew and coconut
girvi	Kannada	Corruption of "gravy"
gujje gasi	Tulu	Jackfruit curry
gutka	Hindi	A chewing tobacco preparation sold in sachets

Hiremath	Proper Noun	A popular family name among the priestly class of the Lingayat caste originally from northern Karnataka
Inglis	Kannada	Corruption of "English"
-ji	Hindi	Suffix to indicate respect
Kadamba Volvo	Noun	Long distance coach operated by the Goa state road transport corporation
kafir	Originally Arabic	A person who disbelieves in Islamic principles (also a racist slur for black Africans)
Kon tume? Kon karya? Kyawn? Ran-deo jao tume...jao... jate-ki-nai? Jate ki NAI? Kya hona tumna?	Dakhani Urdu	Who are you? Who did it? Let it go now. Go away. Will you or won't you go? What do you want from us?

Lingayat	Proper noun	Followers of Lingayatism, a Shaivite community originally from Karnataka
lungi	Kannada	A garment, similar to a sarong, wrapped around the waist and extending to the ankles
matha	Kannada	Caste-specific monastery
mole	Malayalam	Daughter
mudde	Kannada	Dumpling traditionally made of foxtail millet flour
nim unkul	Kannada	Your uncle
odhani	Hindi	A long scarf or veil worn over the shoulders
pai	Portuguese	Father
pakka	Hindi	Solid; well made
panchayat	Most Indian languages	Village council
pao	Portuguese	Bread

pau, poies	Konkani	Kinds of leavened bread sold by *poders*
phorener	Most Indian languages	Corruption of "foreigner"
poder	Konkani	Bread maker/seller
pooja	Most Indian languages	Worship ceremony
pravasi	Kannada	Traveller, also translates as immigrant
raagi	Kannada	Foxtail millet
-ri	Kannada	Suffix to indicate respect
saaru	Kannada	A thin soup typically eaten with *mudde* or rice
salwar	Urdu	Loose trousers held up with drawstrings
santi	Kannada	Weekly market
shoonya	Sanskrit	Zero, nothing
sopo	Konkani	Mortar seat, a typical feature in the verandas of traditional Goan homes

Sudir	Konkani variation of "Shudra"	Lowest of the four varnas of the Hindu social order in India
tangi	Kannada	Younger sister (an affectionate address sometimes used by parents for their daughters)
tharki	Kannada	Corruption of "Turkish", used in the context of towels; the sound by itself translates as "randy"
tiatr	Konkani variation of "teatro", the Portuguese word for theatre	A type of musical theatre popular in the state of Goa
vibhuti	Kannada	Holy ash
yaar	Hindi	Casual address for "friend"

CHARACTERS

- Sylvia Pereira – a young writer
- Cajetan Pereira – "Bhaubaab" – Sylvia's uncle
- Lakshminarayan Shetty – "Lakshmi" – Bhaubaab's neighbour
- Antonio – "Anton" – Cajetan's brother
- Dr Prajapati "Pati-pa" – a university professor; Sujeeth's biological father
- Santhosh – Pati-pa's son
- Bhagirati – Pati-pa's student and later daughter-in-law; also, briefly, Sylvia's colleague
- Bassam – son of Santosh and Bhagirati
- Gandhi-tata – a bonesetter who treats one of Sylvia's husbands
- Sujeeth Jacob Kaniyamparambil – "Juju" – Sylvia's childhood friend
- Shaila Hiremath – Sujeeth's wife
- Rukmini Kulkarni – "Rukku" – daughter of Shaila and Sujeeth's landlord in the village
- Pinjaar Pakirappa – provider of mutton curry to Rukku
- Reshma – Sylvia's childhood friend, later Santosh's lover
- Veena Natarajan and Jacob Kaniyamparambil – Sujeeth's parents and employers of Reshma's mother
- AR – an aspiring writer, Sylvia's fan and email acquaintance
- Nameless man suffering from brain damage that Bhaubaab encounters on the road
- Nine-finger Narayana – Lakshmi in later life

ABOUT THE AUTHOR

Maithreyi Karnoor is the recipient of the Charles Wallace India Trust Fellow in creative writing and translation at Literature Across Frontiers, University of Wales Trinity Saint David. She has been shortlisted for The Lucien Stryk Asian Translation Prize for *A Handful of Sesame*, her translation of a Kannada novel. She is a two-time finalist for The Montreal International Poetry Prize. She lives in Bangalore, India.

Thank you, amma